Law at American River

The fugitives were to meet in American River once they had shaken off the posses. But something went wrong and initially only Fletcher Cody made it back. However, this proved to be an unexpected advantage when, on arrival, Cody the reluctant hero foiled a robbery and murder attempt and earned himself a lawman's badge.

As it turned out, things couldn't have worked better for the remaining outlaws and what they had in mind for the army payroll held at the bank. But, almost too late, they realized others had earmarked the money for themselves. Assassins, stampedes, gunfights and outright murder would decide the outcome.

Law at American River

Jake Douglas

A Black Horse Western

ROBERT HALE · LONDON

© Jake Douglas 2005
First published in Great Britain 2005

ISBN 0 7090 7795 5

Robert Hale Limited
Clerkenwell House
Clerkenwell Green
London EC1R 0HT

Typeset by
Derek Doyle & Associates, Shaw Heath.
Printed and bound in Great Britain by
Antony Rowe Limited, Wiltshire

CHAPTER 1

TWO KINDS OF LAW

The one with the spotted red bandanna masking the lower half of his face threatened to shoot the child unless Sheriff Bill Ritchie cleared the streets and allowed him and his pards to ride out of town.

'God, Bill! *Do* it!' cried a slim, harassed-looking man twisted on to one elbow as he sprawled on the sidewalk outside the bank. One eye was swollen and there was a blood-oozing cut on his right cheek. He turned a pleading face towards the tensed sheriff. 'Bill! For Chrissakes! She's only five years old! Let 'em go! You can chase 'em after! Jesus, it's only money!'

'Not yours, Scanlon!' called one of the men crouching down the sidewalk by the entrance to the saloon, hiding his body as well as he could behind a rain-butt. 'But I got plenty in that bank!'

'Not right now you don't!' called the man with the spotted mask. His voice was showing the strain he was under now. He shook the little girl and made her cry louder and, of course, yelled at her to 'shut up!' – which only made her more frightened. He screwed the gun barrel into the side of her neck and the injured man cried out in anguish.

'Don't! Please, mister, don't!'

'You tell this son of a bitch to clear the streets and let us go, then!' roared the bank-robber, his voice cracking.

Panic was a breath away and most of those watching from safety knew damn well the crazy son of a bitch could kill the girl at any time. They began calling to the bewildered and nerve-racked lawman.

'Let the bastards go, Ritchie!'

'Give 'em right of way! We'll run 'em down later!'

'No, by hell! I got too much money in that bank! Shoot 'em where they stand! Show some guts, Bill!'

'God almighty! That's my daughter out there! Aw, mister, don't hurt her! She's all I got since the wife died! I beg you! Look, you can ride to my ranch – I'll give you directions – take fresh broncs, grub – anythin' you want, just let her go! I catch the hosses an' break 'em myself an' there's some real fast ones in my corrals now—'

'You shut up, Scanlon!' snapped the shaky sheriff. 'Or I'll arrest you for helpin' these damn bandits!'

'Well, do somethin', for God's sake!' shouted Scanlon, right at his wits' end now. 'Do . . . somethin'! Someone. Please!'

The masked man's eyes were wild. His three companions were sweating, edgy, swinging their guns in wild arcs. The man holding the getaway horses was swearing and trying to hold the skittish mounts steady.

'Come on, Bo!' he croaked. 'Come on!'

Something had to go bust here any second.

Then there was a gunshot and the man lying on the boardwalk convulsed and hid his face behind his hand, choking, sobbing, unable to watch his daughter being murdered in front of his eyes.

Men yelled. A woman screamed – and then there were many more gunshots. Scanlon uncovered his eyes slowly and couldn't believe what he was seeing.

The masked man with the spotted bandanna was sprawled on his back in the dust, his forehead smashed in by a bullet. The little girl was hysterical in the dust, screaming and crawling towards her father, one small, grubby hand reaching out for him.

A stranger was crouched behind the sheriff who was down in the dust, hands covering his head. The stranger's sixgun blazed while bullets whistled past him, splinters flying from the false front of the saloon behind him. He bared his teeth and swung his gun slowly and deliberately. One of the other three bandits went down, kicking his last in the gutter. The other two ran for the horses but the getaway man panicked, released their reins, wheeled his own horse and started to rowel it down the street.

The stranger shot down one of the other two and the remaining man threw his hands in the air, shouting: *'Don't shoot! Don't shoot!'* But the stranger shot him anyway, though not fatally. He stepped forward, scooped up the rifle that had fallen from the craven sheriff's hand, levered a shell into the breech and took a quick sight on the fleeing getaway man who had almost reached the end of Main now.

The rifle blasted twice and the horse started to go down first; and then, as the man spilled from the saddle, his body jerked and lost its direction as the second bullet slammed home. He landed on his head and some folk down there claimed they heard his neck snap.

He didn't move after his body stopped skidding through the dust, anyway.

The town was suddenly quiet, dust and gunsmoke mixing to form a dirty cloud that drifted along Main. People began slowly, hesitantly, to show themselves as they crept out of their shelters. All eyes were on the stranger as he tossed the rifle aside, helped the gunwhipped man up off the boardwalk and guided him to where his little girl stood crying, fisting tears from her eyes.

The sheriff, Bill Ritchie, climbed slowly to his feet, his face white and shameful as he turned to the townsfolk he had let down so badly.

A hatless, grey-haired man in shirt-sleeves ran out of the bank, looking wildly around him. He snapped at several clerks making an appearance now. He pointed to the canvas bags the bandits had dropped, stabbing his finger like a knife.

'There! There! Another one there! Get them back inside, into the safe, and *stand guard over them until I come!*'

He turned towards the stranger who was just closing the loading gate of his Colt after reloading. 'Sir! I am Abel Meecham, manager of this fine bank and mayor of this town. I wish to shake your hand for your heroic stand in stopping those bandits ... dead!' He allowed a smile to twitch at his flabby cheek. '*Real* dead!'

But the tall stranger's wolfish, stubbled face didn't change.

'I'm no hero, mister. All I did was what anyone of your yeller-bellied citizens should've done.' He ignored the cries of protest and anger at the insult, set his hard gaze on the sheriff who was dusting himself down with his hat. 'I've seen some yeller snakes in my time, mister, but none as bad as you! You dropped out mighty fast, didn't you.'

'Listen, you!' bristled Bill Ritchie. 'You were lucky, that's all! You played with a little girl's life!'

'You got that wrong, feller,' cut in the stranger, his voice deep and scathing. 'You were the one playin' with her life. I did somethin' about it while you were lookin' for somewhere to run so your own worthless hide didn't get punctured by a bullet.'

'You're right there, stranger!' someone called from the crowd. 'I ain't yaller, but I was too scared to do anythin' but obey that damn robber. Not like this craven bastard we pay to take care of us! Divin' for the dust soon as a gun pointed in his direction!'

He spat at Bill Ritchie but missed. Others hurled insults at the coward and Ritchie forced himself to square his shoulders and glare back.

'Shut up!' he roared. 'What d'you know about it? You were all hidin', playin' it safe! I was the one had to stand out there an' decide! If I'd tried what this – this gun fighter did and it'd gone wrong ... Yeah,

yeah, you can look pale and worried now, but you'd've strung me up to that cottonwood outside the hotel!'

'Damn well oughta do it anyway!' someone called and there were plenty who backed him up, covering their own shame with bluster and finding a ready-made target for the town's anger in the sheriff.

'Yeah! Useless, gutless son of a bitch, Bill! How come it took a stranger to save our money? And little Cathy . . . You did nothin' but drop outta the line of fire!'

The accusations and insults came thick and fast and more than one fist slammed into the sheriff, knocking him to his knees, mouth and nose bleeding. Snarling, he stumbled to his feet, fumbled at his shirt-pocket and tore off the tin star. He hurled it to the ground with a resounding curse.

He glared around at the suddenly quiet crowd.

'There! There's your damn star! Pin it on some-one else! I'm through . . .' He looked around wildly, pointed to the newcomer. 'Him! He's your goddamn hero! Pin the star on him and see what kind of a sher-iff he makes! Now get outta my way. The sooner I shake off the dust of this stinkin' town the better . . .'

He shouldered his way through the crowd and there were a couple who begged him not to be hasty, not to go, that he had been a good sheriff and had made a mistake, that was all, but it could be put right if he'd only reconsider . . .

But he went. Then Ted Scanlon picked up the star, gave it to little Cathy and gestured to her to hand it to the stranger. Tentatively, she walked forward and held out the star towards him but the man seemed to shy away a little.

'Aw, no, wait a minute. I'm no lawman. I don't want no star. I was just lucky. Truth to tell, I feel kinda sick now, thinkin' how I risked young Cathy's life.'

'You *saved* her life, mister!' Scanlon said, backed by most of the crowd now. 'You saved my little girl and I ain't never gonna forget it.' He looked around hopefully. 'Nor is the whole blame town! Am I right, folks? It was your money he saved, too . . .'

He got the reply he wanted and although the stranger was adamant that he didn't want the badge they kept hounding him, until, suddenly, he stopped shaking his head and held out his hand towards the little girl, now riding her father's shoulders. He grinned at her and winked. They cheered as he took the star and pinned it on his shirt.

And that was how Fletcher Cody became the law at American River.

There was a town meeting after the streets were cleaned up, the dead taken to the undertaker's and the wounded bandit treated by Doc Meadows for a bullet in the hip before being locked up in the jail.

Cody was a reluctant hero and sheriff. There were plenty of questions asked, of course – none of which was answered very satisfactorily.

Who was he? Where did he come from? How come he happened to be in American River just as the bank was robbed and Bill Ritchie made a mess of stopping the robbers getting away . . . ? And so on.

It turned out it wasn't the first time the ex-sheriff

had balled things up. There had been a stage robbery a few months back; plenty of tracks, according to the shotgun guard who was the only survivor, but Ritchie got his posse lost in the harsh salt-pan country called Satan's Platter and the robbers had made good their escape. Dad Prendergast, retired now from the railroad, had been guard on a train the spring before last, when bandits had hit, blown the express car with so much dynamite it left only the smouldering flooring and the bogey wheels. It sent splintered planks flying all over the countrywide. One plank had gone clear through the flimsy wall of the caboose and impaled Dad through the shoulder, left him dangling like a side of beef on a hook – it had hurried his retirement. Sheriff Ritchie had led the grim-faced posse that time, too, wreaked havoc with the outlying settlers, accusing them of helping the outlaws, making enemies of almost every one.

With all the squabbling over his roughshod methods and folk downright refusing to renew the posse's mounts because of them, the robbers got away – with several thousand in gold which became untraceable once it was melted down and filtered into the markets across the Rio.

There was talk about Ritchie letting so many of these outlaws get away, suspicion that he might be taking a pay-off. But it was only suspicion – nothing was ever proved.

And he still had a year or so of his term to run. . . .

Now he had resigned – in anger, which he might yet regret. But throwing his star in the dust was good enough for the citizens of American River. And little

Cathy Scanlon was a popular waif who had won the hearts of many townsfolk, some of whom felt mighty guilty about not having done something to save her life.

It would stick in their caws that a stranger had to do it, even though, at the same time, they felt grudgingly grateful.

Ritchie, not only risking Cathy's life, but coming apart at the seams that way – well, it was enough for the town. They were no longer interested in him – only in Fletcher Cody now.

He was nothing special to look at, this Cody. No one would ever mistake him for anything but a drifter. Trail-dusted, worn and patched clothes, boots run over at the heels, battered-looking firearms (maybe from a lot of use, rather than neglect?) and a horse that was more than ready for a curry-combing and a warm stall with oats and hay. All of which the animal received, gratis, from Chink Landon, the livery-stable owner.

Although a room went with the sheriff's job, attached to the rear of the jailhouse, the hotel owner, Morgan Trent, offered a suite comprising bedroom and living-room on the second floor free of charge for the first year of Cody's term. And Cody accepted gratefully, also the new shirt and trousers and a hat from Grady's Emporium, a pair of Mexican-leather riding-boots from the saddler, who also offered to repair and neatsfoot-oil his saddle and riding gear.

Cody accepted all these things readily enough, but when the citizens wanted to take up a collection and buy him a new sixgun and Winchester rifle, he flatly refused.

'Thanks all the same, folks, but I'm kinda used to these old guns.' He slapped the shiny-worn cedar grips of his Colt and hefted the rifle with the rubbed bluing on the barrel and action-plate and the scratched and dented stock. 'Been together a long time and we kinda respect each other now.

The townsfolk were disappointed but nodded their understanding. Later, Wilkie Gann, who claimed to have been a Texas Ranger before they were called Rangers, said Cody's sixgun was a gunfighter's weapon. Looked old and worn but it was oiled slick and smooth and every bullet he took from a belt loop Cody replaced immediately. He even claimed that right under the bottom edge of the butt, where it was hard to see, were two old notches cut into the wood.

That made for a little gossip but not much: Ted Scanlon said what the hell did such a thing matter? Cody had saved not only little Cathy's life, but the whole damn town's money! *That* kind of man could notch his gun or even his pecker if he wanted and he was still a damn sight better sheriff than Bill Ritchie ever was or ever could be.

So the town accepted that. Cody had done them a favour and they made him welcome – until his embarrassment eventually made them realize that he was grateful for their attentions but now was time to *stop*! Right now!

So they let him be and greeted him in friendly manner as he strolled along the streets in his new clothes, smoking a cigarette or an occasional cigarillo, acknowledging each greeting with a short wave or a nod of the head. His hair was long and although the barber told him he could have a haircut and shave any time for free, Cody didn't seem to bother about it. Not right away, at any rate.

His face was that of a man who had seen many things, most of them too shocking or hard for an ordinary family man to accept so calmly. His fists were scarred and plenty big and heavy, yet gentle when he lifted young Cathy and her friends across a muddy gutter or stood them on the top of a rain-butt to admire their frocks or give them candy. His eyes were blue and had a steely glint back in there some-where which a few folk had seen the day he had shot down those bank-robbers.

The wounded man was due to be hanged, but someone shot him through the cell window one night and saved the town a little money. No one ever found out who did it.

Cody enjoyed a few beers with the townsmen, wouldn't let them buy more than one before he slapped his own dollar down on the bar. He liked a hand of poker and he always had a smile and a wink for the painted ladies though no one had yet seen him going upstairs with one. He danced with a couple of townswomen at a church social but left the impression that he had only made a brief appearance because it was expected.

Such things seemed to be of little interest to him.

Then someone noticed that, with all his patrolling of the town, he visited one sector of town more frequently than the rest.

He always stood by the old adobe ruins at the far

end of Main where the tree-line ran out into the dusty trail that led towards Satan's Platter.

Over drinks one night at a corner table in a gloomy part of the saloon, Wilkie Gann spoke up.

'You know what he's doin', don't you?' he said.

A question like that was guaranteed to get all attention focused on him so Wilkie drained his glass, smacked his lips and made a production out of wiping his mouth and blowing his nose and starting to roll a cigarette until Chink Landon got the message and signalled for more beer.

After a good quaff that left white foam clinging to his lopsided moustache, Gann ran his rheumy eyes around the gathered men and said heavily:

'No one ever got a straight answer from our new sheriff about what he was doin' in our town when that bank was robbed. I've seen men like him before, quick with a gun, ridin' easy, but wound up tight inside . . .' He paused again for effect. 'Gents, I'm here to tell you that Sheriff Fletcher Cody is waitin' for somethin' – or some*one*! An' I ain't all that sure it's gonna do this town any good.'

CHAPTER 2

TESTING, TESTING

There had been a couple of drunken brawls, which it hadn't taken long for Cody to break up. The first required only a minor effort, hauling the two drunks apart – they could barely stand unsupported – shaking them and dragging them to the rear door of the saloon. Outside they were deposited against the wall and left to sleep it off.

The second one was a bit more vicious: a fight over one of the bar girls. Broken bottles were involved, a couple of chairs, and boots. When he saw the blood and hanging skin and the way the combatants circled each other with a broken bottle each, Cody knew someone was going to die here, or, at least, require a long spell in hospital.

'Break it up!' he yelled but the men didn't even flick an eye in his direction.

He grabbed one man by the arm and just missed having his face slashed by broken glass. It was enough, especially as the other man took the chance to cut his opponent's back.

Cody whipped out his sixgun, bent the barrel over the head of the closest man, then went for the other. The man lunged at him with his broken bottle and Cody slammed his wrist with his gun, swung again and opened a four-inch cut across the man's fore-head. He didn't bother to catch him as he fell to the sawdust beside his unconscious enemy.

The saloon was quiet as Cody put away his gun, gestured to a small group of cowboys drinking nearby.

'Pack 'em down to the jail for me.'

'Do it yourself,' growled a big redhead. 'Ain't you got a deputy?'

Cody shook his head, icy blue eyes fixed to the redhead's rugged face which showed many scars from past brawls. He knew here was a man ready for a fight at any time.

'I'm askin' you, as a good citizen of American River, to help me.'

'Not me, you ain't. I don't live in this town. You do your own dirty work. You're bein' paid for it.'

Cody held the man's defiant stare a little longer, nodded gently, planning to remember this one, and turned to some other nearby drinkers. They were willing enough and the bleeding men were carried out. As they passed through the batwings, the redhead called:

'Hey, lawman. Them two are part of my crew. What you gonna do with 'em?'

Cody said nothing, pushed through the batwings into the night. As he crossed the boardwalk, seeing the townsmen carrying the unconscious men towards the jail, he heard the rising murmur in the bar – and the pounding boots of a man hurrying towards the entrance.

He stepped to one side, flattening against the wall, drawing his sixgun. The doors smashed open and the redhead staggered out, sixgun in hand, lifting before he had a target. Cody sensed the man's bewilderment as he didn't see the sheriff where he expected to find him; then he said quietly:

'Over here, Red.'

The redhead spun, blinking in the spilled lamplight, then snarled and lifted his gun. Cody slammed his arm aside and the gun thundered, shattering a few slats in the doors, scattering men inside. Cody's gun smashed across Red's ribs and doubled the man over. The sheriff lifted a knee into the contorted face as the man straightened involuntarily and stumbled back, hit him alongside the ear with the side of his gun.

Red dropped and in a minute, Cody had his unconscious form slung over one shoulder and was striding down the street after the two townsmen who were carrying the injured brawlers.

The big man was Red Lindeen, hardcase top hand for the Pitchfork spread, ten miles north-west of town. He was a known troublemaker and had most men cowed. Even those who weren't afraid of him, were reluctant to fight him, because he liked to cripple his opponents permanently. Or kill them.

This information was passed along to Cody by

Chink Landon from the livery.

'Meanest sonuver in the county, Sher'ff. Mel Ryan's been bailin' him outta trouble for years. Keeps him around in case he needs him.'

'For what? Is Red a good cowman?'

Yeah, I reckon he is, but Mel Ryan uses him for . . . other things, too.' Cody waited and it was only a second or two before Chink continued – a man who liked to gossip. 'Mel's a bit of a hardcase hisself. Crowds men off range he decides he needs, and mostly they go and give it to him. If they don't – well, they're likely to have a visit from Red Lindeen. You know what I mean?'

Fletcher Cody nodded slowly. 'Didn't realize there was that kind of trouble here.'

'Hell, ain't much different to most places. Always someone who wants to be king of the dungheap and has to let everyone know it. The range is in your jurisdiction, by the by, Sher'ff.' Chink added this last slyly.

'Yeah, I know. Well, I'll let the trouble come to me for now. I don't know enough about the local set-up yet to go lookin' for it.'

Chink snorted. 'It'll come to you fast enough – now you've gunwhipped Red. And them other two, Laredo and Spanish, them with the broken bottles . . .' He shook his head. 'Sooner you get yourself a deputy to watch your back the better, Cody.'

The sheriff sensed that the warning was well meant and figured he would take note of it – but he didn't want a deputy just yet. He wanted to make his own assessment of this town, get the lie of the ground, before he made up his mind about what he would do next: work with a deputy of his own choosing, or simply move on.

It depended on what American River was prepared to offer – knowingly or otherwise.

The next time someone decided to put him to the test they tried to kill him.

Happened this way.

It was on one of Cody's casual night patrols. He just took a stroll around town before turning in, quietened down a few drunks – a sharp word was usually enough now after the way he had put down Red Lindeen – and dragged the odd unconscious ranny snoring off his booze in the middle of the street or other precarious place to the boardwalk.

As usual, he went to the adobe ruins and lit a last cigarillo before returning to the hotel and his suite of rooms. He kept staring out at the distant thin silver line marking the edge of the Satan's Platter salt-pans.

The time was up. They had arranged to wait for each other no more than a week at the most in American River. This was the last day and still no sign of him. . . .

Cody flicked the butt of the cigarillo away into the night, watching the brief burst of sparks as it hit the ground. *Things were different now, though – he had taken on the job of administering law here. He could walk away from it at any time, of course, but there was nothing to be gained by that – he reckoned he would wait now. Things might still work out as they had planned. . . .*

As he turned his gaze away from the ruins towards the town again, his peripheral vision detected a slight bright spot in a dark angle of the crumbling wall where there had been nothing but shadow before.

Instantly, Cody dropped to one knee, his sixgun palming up as flame daggered the darkness and a handful of adobe exploded not a foot from his head. His upper body twisted and the Colt bucked against his hand in two rapid shots. A man grunted and the next flare of flame from the black corner was angled high as the gunman spilled drunkenly over the broken edge of the wall. The man hung there moaning, and Cody threw himself sideways, full length, rolling in towards the adobe.

As he had suspected there had been a second man waiting in the ruins and a large chunk of wall exploded in dust and grit as a shotgun thundered. Near-deafened by the closeness of the Greener, Cody twisted around on the ground, braced his elbow and hammered three shots into the angle of the wall as the shotgun's second barrel discharged with a murderous roar.

He felt the wind of hot buckshot carving the air just above his head and then there was a clatter of metal. A dark shape reared up and staggered across the stars in a brief drunken dance before crashing headlong.

Cody waited, heart hammering, thumbing fresh loads into his gun's cylinder by feel, watching for a third man. But they had figured two would be enough.

One was Laredo, the least hurt from the fight with broken bottles. Spanish, who had been cut in the back and had a wrist damaged, was still in Doc

Meadows infirmary. The other man was a drifter Cody had seen lounging around town.

He wondered if the bushwhack idea had been Laredo's or Red Lindeen's – or even this Mel Ryan's, whom he hadn't yet had the pleasure of meeting.

But he would soon fix that and when the townsmen came to see what all the shooting was about he told them to carry the dead men into town, but to tell the undertaker he wanted both bodies wrapped in canvas and he would pick them up in the morning.

'Oh – and tell Chink Landon I want a buckboard made available,' he called as he turned back towards town, aiming to get a good night's sleep.

Tomorrow could be a mighty interesting day.

Mel Ryan, a hard-muscled man just under six feet tall, torso bulging his shirt, was branding calves in the lower ranch yard when he saw the dust of a vehicle coming down the trail from town.

Mel straightened, thumbed back his hat and squinted. There was a flash from the driving seat of the buckboard. Red Lindeen released the calf that had just had the Pitchfork brand burned into its hide.

'Well, well, well,' he said. 'Do b'lieve we're about to be visited by the new sheriff, boss.'

Ryan frowned. He was a man in his early forties, had a craggy face. His grey eyes narrowed. He scrubbed a hand across the dark frontier moustache above his wide mouth.

'Wonder what he wants . . . ?'

Red glanced at his boss sharply. *Had he detected a*

slight edge of worry in Ryan's words?

By that time Cody was swinging the vehicle through the gate and a couple of cowhands working on the fence nearby straightened stiff backs as an excuse to rest and stare at him. The sheriff hauled rein. His mount, a big black-brown gelding, tied on to the tailboard, skidded to a halt as the team came to a stop.

'Well, what we got here?' Ryan said, approaching, hauling off the dirt-stiffened work gloves. He tensed as Cody reached back and flipped aside the square of canvas covering the bodies of Laredo and the drifter.

'How about these?'

Ryan glanced at the dead men, flicked sober eyes to Cody.

'I know who they are. Dunno you.'

'Red knows who I am.'

'Fletcher Cody, he calls himself, boss,' Red said with a sneer, rubbing at his sore ribs. 'Stopped a bank robbery and they gave him Bill Ritchie's badge.'

'Mmmm. Heard about that.'

'Long before Red told you,' Cody said and Ryan smiled crookedly.

'Well, what you want? I ain't no undertaker.'

'They tell me they're your men.'

'Laredo was. That drifter's just a roustabout, pickin' up a dollar here and there.'

'Figured that. My guess was Laredo, or someone he worked for, paid him that dollar or two to bushwhack me at the adobe ruins.'

Their gazes met and locked, two hard-willed tough men, neither willing to give an inch. Ryan shrugged.

'Why would you think I might be involved? I got

no beef with you – yet.'

'Lookin' forward to it, are you?' Cody climbed down from the driving-seat and walked around the team to face Ryan.

They were about the same height but Ryan was heavier, bulging with muscle from years of ranch work. At the same time, though appearing slimmer, Cody had the easy resilience of a rawhide whip; it showed in every motion, even when he started to build a cigarette.

'You employ some hard *hombres*, Ryan.' Cody flicked his eyes towards Red, who gave him a sneer.

'Ranchin' this country's a hard job. Needs tough men.'

'And law to match.' Cody lit up, staring through the first exhalation of smoke at the rancher.

Ryan frowned. 'You ridin' me? Why you comin' down on me like this? You ain't been here but five minutes and—'

'And I've already tangled with three of your men. Mebbe four.' Cody jerked his head towards the dead drifter. 'They weren't much of a challenge – if they were meant to test me.'

Ryan placed his hands on his hips. 'Mister, I don't give a good goddamn about you. If you tangled with some of my men while they were on the booze, it's got nothin' to do with me. And I'll go on record by tellin' you that I resent you accusin' me this way.'

'Duly noted, Ryan. Hope you'll take note, too.' He went to the tailgate and untied his mount, stepping easily into the saddle. 'Could be we'll see each other again.'

'You keep on bein' hardnosed like this and I can practically guarantee it!'

Cody smiled crookedly. 'Be seein' you, then.'

As he swung his horse and started for the gate, Ryan called: 'Hey! What about Landon's buckboard?'

'Have one of your men return it. I paid for one hour's hire. Anythin' over that it's on your slate.'

He lifted a hand casually and spurred off. Ryan glared after him, face tight.

'Son-of-a-*bitch*!' said Red Lindeen, staring. 'You b'lieve that Cody . . . ?'

Ryan didn't answer for a long moment, then nodded gently.

'Yeah, I do. But why come down on me like that? He's proddin' hard and seems to be enjoyin' it. I think this Mr Fletcher Cody needs some lookin' into . . .' He stopped suddenly and snapped his head up watching as Cody set the black-brown gelding to the slope of the trail as it rose over the hogback. 'Wait a minute! Fletcher Cody – or Cody Fletcher?'

He was looking at Lindeen now and Red blinked, puzzled, shrugged his shoulders. 'Says his name's Fletcher Cody, boss. He—'

'He *says*! But somethin' rings a bell way back in my head. I get a feel'n' of Utah? Mebbe Wyomin'? No! *Dakota*! That's where it was . . . Deadwood. Three years back. Was a wild bunch operatin' up there, led by a feller called – what the hell was his name? Yeah, Luther Rennie, the Mad Preacher. Seems he'd read from the Bible over some of the folk he killed on raids or in hold-ups. They broke up when the army moved in. I recollect a name on the wanted list they posted for the gang members; sure it was Cody Fletcher!'

Red said tiredly: 'this feller's Fletcher Cody.'

'Mebbe. Cody Fletcher was a lawman, till someone raped his wife, left her for dead. She lived long enough to tell him it was an army captain. Fletcher went out and killed him and they put a bounty on him, so he joined Rennie's wild bunch . . .'

'Why you think it's the same feller? You ever see him?'

Ryan shook his head. 'Heard about him. Tough lawman liked to crowd folks, make 'em toe the line . . .'

Red shrugged sceptical, and Ryan's face went hard.

'I'm a man who follows his hunches, Red, you know that. So we tread easy for a spell, till we find out more.'

Red nodded but it was plain by the look on his face just what he thought of his boss's theory.

Then a slim figure came out of the shadowed doorway of the barn.

'What'd I tell you, Mel? Said he was a hardnosed bastard – and you ask me, we've got ourselves a whole passel of trouble.'

Ex-sheriff Bill Ritchie bent his head into the match flame and blew a plume of smoke towards the rancher, a mocking look on his narrow face.

Ryan glared. 'If we have, it's because of you!'

'Hell, I done what I had to. I – I admit I got the wind up when Bo Bantry set his gun on me. But no one expected this Cody to step in and shoot him. Bantry was the problem. Him and Cody.'

'Well, I'll end it!' Ryan grated. 'No damn drifter's gonna spike my guns.'

CHAPTER 3

SURVIVOR

Sheriff Fletcher Cody was working at his desk – sitting there reading wanted dodgers, anyway – when a townsman burst into the office, holding the street door ajar.

'Sher'ff! You better come quick!' he panted.

Cody lifted his eyes from the dodgers.

'Why?' he asked.

'Jim Borden just rode in from his spread. Says he sighted what looked like a man out on Satan's Platter.'

While the man caught his breath, Cody stood slowly. 'What? *Looked* like a man . . . ?'

'Yeah! Hard to see with all that – glare, you know? Jim's gettin' on, eyesight ain't much these days, but he says it could be – a man.'

'Walkin'?'

'Er – well, I guess. He din' say.'

'So he rode on in here,' Cody said grimly, reaching down his hat. 'And if it is a man, he could be

29

dead by the time someone gets to him.'

'Well, like I said, Jim's pretty old now and he couldn't do much. You want a posse?'

'No, I don't want a posse. But I want Doc Meadows on stand-by. You go tell him. And I'll grab a spare horse from the livery and go see for myself.'

He grabbed his already-filled saddle canteen and a spare hat that had been hanging on a wall peg when he took over Ritchie's office.

Minutes later he was riding out past the adobe ruins, watched by townsfolk who had heard the news from Jim Borden himself – and the oldster planned to get a couple more drinks yet out of his bar audience before they figured he had little more to tell them than what the townsman had told Cody: that he had glimpsed a dark shape through the haze and heat-shimmer from the salt-pans. Might have been an animal or a man crawling on all fours.

Jim, who led a pretty boring life these days on his lonely spread, figured it wouldn't hurt to stir things up a little and say it definitely was a man he'd seen – and walking. He turned back into the saloon bar, a few hangers-on throwing more questions at him. . . .

But he was more correct than he knew.

It was a man Cody found out there. And he was in a bad way. He was so dusted with salt and alkali that Cody couldn't tell whether he was white, black or yellow. Until he set the canteen to the split and blistered lips and some of the water splashed and washed away a little of the salt.

There was a dark coppery skin underneath.

Cody sat back on his heels as he pulled the canteen away from the eager mouth.

'Take it easy, *amigo*. You'll be OK now . . .'

The man's hat fell off and Cody saw the raven-black hair pulled into a pony-tail at the back. He splashed water over the high-cheekboned face and the matted eyelashes started to open. He rubbed them gently with wet fingers, massaging away the gluey matter, a mixture of glare-produced tears and alkali and deadly strain. This man must have been out there for some time: three – four days at least.

'Lose your horse?' Cody asked and after a time the man nodded, eyes shut again now. 'You – walked?'

Again the nod and then a harsh whisper. 'Had . . . to . . .'

'Uh-huh. Pretty desperate. Any one after you?'

Another long pause. 'Not . . . now.'

'I see. You shake 'em, or . . . ?'

'Or.'

Cody started to speak but heard a horse whiny and he spun, hand streaking to his gun butt. There were four riders coming towards him from the direction of town: prying ratfinks, though he gave them the benefit of the doubt and thought maybe they had come out of humanitarian motives.

Chink Landon was one and he spoke curtly to the sheriff.

'If you hadn't left that buckboard out at Pitchfork a few days ago, I might've had one left to load this feller in to.'

'Take it up with Ryan, Chink. . . .'

One of the other townsmen, a saloon loafer, was

kneeling beside the survivor and suddenly reared back.

'Aw, hell, it's only some Injun! An' we rid all the way out here just for that!'

Cody was standing. He placed a boot against the loafer's shoulder and thrust, spilling the protesting man into the bitter salt-and-alkali dust.

'He's not an Injun, Stew. He's a *man* – and he needs help.'

Stew got up, dusting himself down and spitting.

'He don't get none from me! Day I help an Injun there'll be icicles in hell!'

'Then get the hell back to town.'

'Hey, you can't order me around like that . . .'

Cody's face was hard and it took only one look for Stew to swear under his breath and climb back on his horse.

'You fellers comin'?' he asked the others.

'They're gonna help me,' Cody said and the others knew they had no choice. . . .

Doc Meadows was waiting at his infirmary. His wife had prepared a bed for the desert survivor. The only other bed in the small infirmary was occupied by Spanish, the man who had been cut on his back by Laredo's bottle and who had had his wrist slammed by Cody's gun barrel. He was a mean-looking cuss with an axe-blade face and glittering eyes that followed Cody's every movement. But he said nothing as the sheriff stood by and watched Meadows and his wife go to work on the Indian.

'Man's dehydrated badly. Touch of heat-stroke,

too,' the medic told the sheriff. 'He'll be a week before he's anywhere near back to normal. A few more hours and he'd've been dead.

'He's pretty tough, Doc.'

Meadows glanced at Cody quickly. 'You know him?'

'He's an Indian,' Cody said. 'They're always ten times tougher than a white man. Because they don't give up as easily as a white man does.'

'Eyewash!' said Spanish. 'Injuns don't give up 'cause they just don't know no better!'

'Reason don't matter,' Cody told him bleakly. 'Not if it pulls you through . . .'

Spanish curled a lip. 'You an Injun-lover – as well as lawman?'

'Give you somethin' else to fire up your hate, Spanish,' Cody said easily. Doc Meadows frowned and said quietly and a little worriedly:

'Easy, Sheriff. That man's dangerous. Likes to use a knife—'

'Or a broken bottle if a knife's not handy. Yeah, Doc, I got his measure. You look after this feller, call me when he can talk and tell me what he was doin' out there in Satan's Platter, OK?'

The doctor said he would do as Cody asked. The sheriff paused by Spanish's bed, the man tensing as he saw those cold eyes.

'When's this one due for discharge, Doc?'

'Any time. Ryan won't pay for his care and I doubt he'll have two cents to rub together himself.'

'Well, you head on back to Pitchfork, Spanish, when Doc kicks you out. If I find you in town, I'll lock you up.'

'Who you think you are!'

Cody grinned coldly, made a gun out of his fore-finger and thumb and flicked the latter like a gun hammer dropping.

Dr and Mrs Meadows couldn't be sure, but they thought Spanish's swarthy skin took on a greyish-white colour as the sheriff strode out of the infirmary.

The town council called a special meeting that night. The mayor, banker Abel Meecham, looked uncom-fortable as he told Cody that there had been complaints about Cody's high-handed methods, bossing folk around, making them toe the line. Even Mel Ryan, a tough man himself, had complained that Cody had tried to intimidate him.

Cody laughed briefly.

'The day someone like Mel Ryan's intimidated by someone like me is gonna be a day to remember, Mayor.'

'This is no laughing matter, Cody,' Meecham said stiffly. 'We ... wouldn't want to think that we ... made a mistake in making you sheriff.'

Cody spread his hands. 'You just say, Mayor, and you can have this badge. I only took the job because I was near broke. But whatever a job pays, I do the best I can. Point of honour with me.'

'Not only pays good,' said the storekeeper stiffly, 'but we gave you new clothes, a free suite of rooms and—'

'That's OK. You can have it all, if you insist – I'll just move on. I only stopped by for few beers in the first place ... Never even got 'em before them bandits came rushin' outta the bank. Got someone in mind for the job?'

That unsettled the council. They had to admit that Cody might use rough methods but the town *had* been quieter and a lot tamer: the womenfolk felt safer since he had taken over the lawman's job. But the council members were elected and when they had complaints from the citizens they had to be seen to be at least *trying* to do something about it or, come voting time, they would be out of a part-time job which paid a generous expense allowance that was rarely – if ever – questioned.

'Look, Sheriff – Fletcher,' Meecham said with a forced grin, glancing around at his colleagues. 'We know this town needs cleaning up some. Bill Ritchie kind of let things go a bit. But the citizens aren't the problem. It's the trail hands or the ranch crews, the people who come in for a few days of wild celebration and turn American River into a small corner of hell. The citizens resent being told off by you when these other fellers are the ones who give the town a bad name. The townsfolk expect – and rightly so – some leniency. But you come down hard on anyone who steps over the line . . .'

'This council made up the town ordinance,' Cody reminded them. 'I'm just doing my job by enforcing it.'

That caused a discussion but it was obvious that the council members were glad Cody was no longer talking about – or threatening – resignation.

'Listen, perhaps Cody needs a deputy,' suggested Landon. 'I mean, he's doin' a big job by himself and if he had someone to handle the night patrols and so on . . .'

'You people want to appoint me a deputy?' Cody asked and saw by their quick reaction that that was exactly what they wanted to do. Appoint a man who would report back to them, countermand orders or smooth over any of the townsfolk Cody might rub the wrong way. . . .

'Gents, you gave me a job to do and now I'm thinkin' that all you wanted was for me to do it *your* way? Right?'

Yeah, but they hadn't figured Cody would be so independent.

'It's to everybody's advantage,' said Dallas Westermann; he ran the largest saloon and would want a wide-open town. But the smile was wiped from his face when Cody shook his head.

'I take on a job, I do it the best I know how. Don't know no different, always been that way. But gents, I will take your advice and hire me a deputy.'

They grinned at each other; they would be able to control Cody after all . . . Again the smiles disappeared like someone blowing out a lantern as Cody added: 'I got just the man.'

'Er – well, we have our own thoughts on this, Sheriff . . .' Meecham spoke again and the others murmured agreement. 'But who did you have in mind?'

'Man name of Starbuck.'

The council exchanged puzzled glances. 'Never heard of him,' snapped Westermann. 'Who's this Starbuck, Cody?'

36

'The feller we hauled outta Satan's Platter the other day.'

Stunned silence. Then Chink Landon exclaimed: 'That – that *Injun?*'

'Yeah. Can't pronounce his Injun name, but he answers to Starbuck and he's lookin' for work. I'll go tell him he's got the job and swear him in.'

They all began to bluster but Cody ignored them and went out into the night.

The doctor said he wasn't sure that the Indian was quite ready for discharge yet, but Cody merely pushed past. 'Let's ask him, Doc,' he said. 'It's important.'

Meadows hurried after Cody.

'Look, Sheriff, I've heard about how tough you are but you are not going to come in here and bully me in my own infirmary. That I will not stand for, no matter who tries it . . .'

'No bullying intended, Doc, but I've got to move fast.' Cody paused near the Indian's bed; the man appeared to be sleeping. The bed that had been occupied by Spanish was empty. Cody looked at the medic. 'I dunno how you stand on this, Doc, but the council are gettin' cold feet about havin' given me the sheriff's job. I'm too rough on the citizens, they say, and they have a complaint from Mel Ryan . . .'

'Ryan! By God, it's a red-letter day if that arrogant cowman takes any kind of legal step towards the council or anyone else!'

'He's just sounding off. Doc, they want to appoint their own deputy, someone to keep an eye on me, throw a rope on me and hogtie me when it suits *them.*'

Meadows gave him a speculative glance.

'You have your own reasons for wanting a free hand, I take it.'

Cody shrugged. 'I don't like bein' crowded, told how to do work that's essentially a one-man job. They gave me a set of rules and now that I'm enforcin' them, if it don't suit them or one of their friends is offended, then they want to pull me up short.'

Meadows almost smiled. 'And that would never do for Fletcher Cody, would it . . . ?'

'Not by a damn sight . . .'

The Indian sat up.

'Can't a man get any sleep around here?'

'That's the first grammatically correct sentence I've heard you say!' exclaimed the medic.

Starbuck grunted. 'Can recite the Gettysburg Address word for word. Anyway, Doc, the Cherokee Nation is the only North American Indian tribe to have its own alphabet, you know that?' He flicked his dark gaze to Cody without waiting for a reply. 'What's up?'

Cody told him, concluded with: 'Thought you might like the deputy's job.'

Starbuck remained silent.

'Why did you pick him, Sheriff?' asked Meadows.

'He's gotta be mighty tough to've survived Satan's Platter, Doc. I've a feelin' I'm gonna need that kind of man to help me here.'

'If you feel the job's beyond you . . .'

Cody's face was sober now. 'You don't figure an

Indian deputy'll go down well in this town?'

Meadows smiled. 'What d'you think?'

'I think this town's about to be a mite shook up.'

Meadows chuckled this time. 'That's what I figured you'd say. But it all depends on you, Mr Starbuck . . . ?'

The Indian shrugged. 'I'll take the job.'

'Now why did I have a feeling you were going to say exactly that?' Meadows turned to Cody. 'I think perhaps you'll be good for this town, Cody. At least, I'm sure that it'll never be the same again after you two get through with it!'

Outside in the cool night, as they walked slowly back towards the hotel side by side, Cody said:

'They're watchin' us.'

'OK. You gonna stick, then?'

'Hell, yeah. Better than the original plan. Bein' the law in American River we're in a mighty fine position to find out what we want to know.' He gestured to the hotel. 'Here we are.'

The Indian stopped at the foot of the steps.

'They won't let me in here.'

'Likely won't want to, but you're my guest so we'll just have our few words with the night clerk and the manager if we have to, then go upstairs to my rooms and you can tell me what the hell kept you from gettin' here a week ago like we arranged.'

CHAPTER 4

THE LAWMEN

Once in the suite of rooms and settled into a chair in the parlour, smoking one of Cody's cigarillos, Starbuck spoke.

'I got the best excuse in the world for bein' late: I was in jail. Place called Basket Creek.'

'The hell were you doin' in a dump like that? That's miles off the trail I figured you'd take.'

Starbuck blew a long plume of smoke, staring at the ceiling.

'There was this little gal on a freight wagon headin' that way and I sort of followed 'em in. Mistook her for an Arapahoe. She was a Mexican bred, and her family had been wiped out by Comanches. An Injun was an Injun to her and she hollered before I realized my mistake. She tripped me as I ran down the stairs and they were waitin' at the bottom, guns out and lynch rope all ready.'

Cody smoked slowly, waiting.

'Decided they'd wait till daylight to string me up –

give everyone a better view. But the jailer come a leetle too close to the bars and I was able to grab his keys just before he fell back out of reach. Only way I could throw the posse was by crossin' that damn desert. Near killed me.'

'But you got here and you're wearin' a deputy's badge now, and I'm the sheriff. Makes things easier than we originally planned.

'Dunno about that. We just had one helluva fuss down in the lobby.'

Cody smiled slowly, remembering the way the night clerk had panicked when he had been told that Starbuck would be staying as Cody's guest. The man called Morgan Trent the manager, a sly-looking type with slicked-down hair and shifty eyes.

'Now, Sheriff, you surely know better than this! Man, this is a frontier town, not fifty miles from the border! We're in the heart of Indian country here and you expect . . .' He was lost for words, gestured to Starbuck and shook his head. 'Sorry, I'll have to ask you both to leave.'

'Ask away,' Cody said. 'But send someone up with a bottle of bourbon soon as you can, OK?'

'Wait!' Trent's voice was almost a yelp as the sheriff and his new deputy started for the stairs. 'God almighty, Sheriff, you can't do this to me! I've got the hotel's reputation to think of!'

'Yeah, well, I can savvy that. Tell 'em you got a genuine decorated war hero stayin' here – and think about this: you'll have two bona fide lawmen as guests, right on the spot in case of trouble—'

'This hotel does not have – trouble!' Trent raised

up on to his toes with indignation.

Cody grinned without humour.

'But s'pose, just s'pose, when the next trail herd comes in that word gets around the hotel is runnin' its own line of exclusive – ladies, shall we say?'

'I've never done . . . !' Trent's protest almost choked him, his eyes bulging. But then he saw the set of Cody's jaw and the Indian staring at the floor. His voice was barely audible when he said: 'You would-n't!'

Cody shrugged. '*I* wouldn't, Mr Trent, but – hell, who knows where such rumours start – or finish?'

Trent swallowed. 'I'll remember this, Cody! You're riding high right now, but comes the time for your appointment to be renewed – well, I'll be a member of the town council soon, my application is up for consideration right now—'

'Good luck, Mr Trent,' Cody said over his shoulder as he started up the stairs with Starbuck. 'Oh – don't forget that bourbon – and make it bonded. None of your rotgut.'

'This hotel does not serve rot . . .' Trent cut off his protest, threw up his arms and nodded to the sweating, white-faced clerk, handing him a key. 'Take him up a bottle of my bourbon – and make sure it goes on his bill. Though God knows I have little hope of ever collecting. . . .'

Now Cody poured them two more drinks in his parlour and they sipped and smoked in silence for a short time.

'Heard it was Bantry's bunch,' Starbuck said at last.

Cody nodded. 'Recognized Bo. Still wearin' that damn spotted red bandanna. Might just as well have had a tag round his neck with his name on it.'

'His brother, Big Joe, was the smart one. Bo never had enough brains to run that outfit after Joe died.'

'Fool grabbed a little girl and was threatening' to kill her 'less the sheriff let 'em ride out.' Cody frowned. 'Stupid move, even for Bo, and Ritchie was mighty nervous. Mind, no one was backin' him and the Bantrys were ready to fight. That'd scare a lot of men.'

The Indian looked up sharply. 'The townsmen weren't sidin' with Ritchie . . . ?'

'Didn't appear to be. Figured it must've taken everyone by surprise, caught Ritchie flat-footed, too.'

'And you just had to buy in.'

'Well, couldn't let a damn fool like Bo Bantry and his men cut our legs from under us. Even if he didn't know he was doin' it.'

Starbuck nodded. 'World's gotta be a better place without that bunch. But why take the law badge?'

'Told you – gives us the inside edge. Meecham is gonna be in a sweat and he'll want all the back-up he can get now the Bantrys almost pulled off that robbery. Ritchie wouldn't've been much good, not with that yellow streak.'

'If it was the real thing.'

Cody frowned. 'Been thinkin' about it and I've asked a few quiet questions about Ritchie. Seems he's been a good enough lawman, favoured a few, of course, like Mel Ryan's cowhands and so on, but generally kept the place in some sort of order.

Though Meecham said at that council meetin' that Ritchie'd "let things slide", whatever that means.'

'Was turnin' a blind eye to some of the rough stuff, mebbe. Likely had his hand out. Or was dealin' with the likes of the Bantrys.'

'Ye-ah, could be. Well, he quit town, so he's not a worry now.'

'When's it gonna happen . . . ?'

'Yet to find out. But I reckon I'll be next to know after Meecham, once he gets word. I mean – I'm the law here now.' He smiled crookedly. 'With a genuine Cherokee for deputy.'

Starbuck winced a little as he shifted his weight in his chair, still suffering a few stabs of pain from his desert ordeal.

'I tell you, I got no notion to have to cross that damn alkali again. Once was one time too many.'

'Well, it's the best escape route but I've been lookin' over the survey maps and there's two other ways we might try – but only if we have to.'

'Anythin' but that damn desert.'

'Thought you knew all about deserts. Recollect you talkin' about it when those Rebs cornered us at Hathaway's Landin' and we'd run out of ammo and figured we'd reached the end of the line . . .'

'And you jumped at the idea of me knowin' deserts and bullied me into leadin' the troop across them badlands south-west of the Landin'. Yeah, I recollect all right!'

'Got you a medal, didn't it? First Injun to win a white man's medal in the war. Hell, you were even proud of it – for a spell.'

'Didn't do me no good: wouldn't even serve me in a saloon. And I still get the shivers when I think of them badlands, Cody.'

'It was tough but we made it, didn't we? The Rebs dropped out early and you got us through, Star. I was kind of countin' on you to do the same with Satan's Platter, figured any posse comin' after us – and there's sure to be at least one – would give up and reckon us as good as dead.'

Starbuck shook his head slowly.

'Damn you, Cody! I know when you take that tone of voice you ain't gonna let up on me till I say I'll do it!'

'Well, you made it once and – I guess you could say I saved your life . . .' Cody examined his fingernails.

Starbuck glared, then grinned when he saw the slight movement of Cody's mouth.

'You son of a bitch!' He thrust out his glass again. 'Come on – fill it up. And let's drink to our success.'

Cody refilled the glasses and winked as he held his up to his mouth. 'Never a doubt about it, Star. Never a doubt about it.'

Mel Ryan, like most of the town of American River, couldn't believe it when told that Cody had sworn in a full-blood Cherokee as deputy.

'Christ, they'll string him up! Cody, too!'

'Save us a problem if they did,' said Bill Ritchie.

He and Ryan were sitting on the porch after supper and one of the cowhands who had gone to town to pick up the mail had brought back the news about Starbuck.

Ryan pursed his lips. 'This Cody makes me uneasy, Bill. Things were OK long as you toted the sheriff's badge but now . . . Anyway, why in *hell* did you let 'em give the star to Cody?'

'You think I had a choice?' Ritchie was edgy now at the question.

'They say you turned yellow when Bantry put a gun to the kid's head,' Ryan said softly, his gaze penetrating.

Ritchie swore softly. 'Damn it, Bantry and those loco men of his had been smokin' the Mexican weed, and boozin' it up. Figured they could beat the whole blame world and pulled the robbery in full daylight to prove it. Caught me flatfooted, and then when Bo gunwhipped Scanlon and grabbed little Cathy . . .' He shook his head. 'The town would've killed me if anythin' had happened to her so I acted scared, just hopin' like hell Bo wouldn't take the kid along when he went.'

'I hear your "actin" was pretty damn good,' Ryan allowed with quiet insinuation. 'Convinced most everyone.'

Ritchie stood, angry, fists clenched. 'OK! I *was* scared! Hell, you ever been on the wrong end of Bo Bantry's gun when he's drugged and full of booze? Damn right I was shakin'. But I didn't figure the town'd turn agin me when I got mad an' told 'em to stick their lousy badge.'

'And made a whole heap of trouble for us.'

Ritchie sat down slowly. 'Well, I just didn't figure a drifter like Cody would take the badge; figured that the council would have to give it back to me . . .'

'Well, it's done and I hear Cody's upset a few townsfolk as well as the council. They might yet fire him and then we won't have to worry about him. But now he's gone and hired himself this Injun deputy.'

'Yeah, and he ain't just any ordinary Injun. He's got a Medal of Honour from the War.' As Ryan stared in disbelief, Ritchie half-smiled. 'First of only half a dozen given to Injuns. This Starbuck led a Yankee troop to safety across them badlands near Hathaway's Landin'. The Rebs near died chasin' 'em, gave up.'

'Well, he's well south of the old Mason-Dixon now and a full-blood Cherokee to boot. A bit of brass on a ribbon ain't gonna make folk love him.'

'Guess not. Mebbe we can use that, turn 'em agin Cody so much they *make* him turn in his badge.'

Ryan smiled crookedly. 'You want that sheriff's job back bad, don't you, Bill.'

'We-ell, I did all right when I had it. Folk was used to me. I got me a lotta – concessions, you know what I mean? Whorehouses, saloons, diners, just about anythin'.'

'They might've been used to you, Bill, but they didn't like you. Now they've seen your yellow steak, you'll never wear that star again in American River.'

Ritchie was angry now.

'No? You reckon not? You think I can't handle some drifter like Cody?'

'No, I don't think you could handle him. Not you and Spanish together, and *he* wants Cody so bad he's honed his knife down till it's no thicker than a knittin' needle.' Ryan said it quietly, yet his words prodded the ex-sheriff.

47

Ritchie was too mad to notice right then that he was being *told* what to do, but it would come to him later. Like when he saw Spanish *still* preparing his blade to drink Cody's blood. *He would figure it out just fine.*

Cody didn't want Starbuck to take the night patrol.

The Indian hadn't been well received in town, as was to be expected, but Cody figured there was enough open hostility to make it dangerous for him to be walking the streets of American River during the cold dark hours.

Dallas Westermann at the saloon refused to serve Starbuck a drink even when he was with Cody.

'Read your ordinance, Cody,' Westermann told the sheriff coldly. 'Says no Injuns or Negroes allowed in this bar.'

'That'd be your contribution when it was bein' drawn up, would it, Dallas?' Cody asked mildly.

The saloon owner shrugged. 'It's been passed as part of the ordinance, so you can't make me serve him – and, fact is, I want him outta here within the next ten seconds.' Westermann looked steadily at Cody. 'What're you drinkin', Sheriff?'

'Give me a bottle of bonded bourbon – and none of the stuff that's not true to label.'

'We don't serve rotgut if it's labelled as somethin' different,' Westermann said stiffly, reaching back to the shelves. He slammed a bottle in front of Cody. 'Two dollars.'

Cody said nothing, drew the cork with his teeth, swigged from the neck. He spat out the burning liquid almost as soon as it filled his mouth. Westermann jumped back as some of the spray caught him.

'Hey!'

'That the best you've got?'

'Best in the bar,' Dallas said smugly.

'How about your private stock?'

'That's what it is – *private* stock.'

Cody nodded and glanced at Starbuck who still stood impassively beside him.

'Like to try it, Star? Wouldn't recommend it, but see what you think.'

'Hey, hey! He don't drink in here, I said!'

Westermann's face was dark with rage and some of the drinkers growled, too; they didn't want to drink in the same bar as an Indian. Starbuck took the bottle, swigged, spat out the liquid on to Westermann's shirt-front.

'You're right, Cody. Pig's swill. Though I wouldn't give this to any self-respectin' pig.' Then Star grinned, looking at the furious saloon man as he wiped down his shirt. 'Hell, too late! I already give some to a pig an' didn't realize it!'

That was it. Westermann reached under the bar for his billy and started to leap over the counter. Cody lifted a hand, caught him in the chest and thrust him back hard. Westermann hit the shelves and half a dozen bottles shattered as he sprawled on the floor. He started to get up but Cody leaned across, pointing his sixgun at him.

'Stay put, Dallas. – I could throw you in jail for attackin' a duly sworn deputy, but I'll just close you down for now—'

'You *what*!' Westermann came up, bug-eyed.

Drinkers were getting to their feet now. Starbuck drew his pistol and no one moved although they looked mighty mad.

'It's in the ordinance. "Any place of refreshment serving substandard food or *liquor* with an eye to making unfair profit shall be closed down and called upon to show cause in a court of law. Penalty: a fine of two hundred dollars and/or jail for the proprietor . . ." '

Westermann stared. 'That ain't in the ordinance!'

'Will be when I amend it and put it to the council.'

'Like hell it will!'

'Well, just in case, Dallas, you get the customers out of here and close for the night. We'll settle this tomorrow, or the next day. Maybe next week. But you stay close until we do.'

It caused uproar but Cody stopped it by firing a shot into the roof, 'accidentally' clipping the wagon-wheel chandelier with its two dozen oil-lamps on the rim, smashing several.

'Start clearin' the bar, gents!'

There was a lot more shouting and cursing but after a couple more shots into the sawdusted floor, the drinkers began to shuffle their way out. Westermann glared.

'Just so a damn Injun can get himself a drink!'

Cody raised his eyebrows, looking at Starbuck.

'Oh? You want a drink, Star?'

'Wouldn't drink in this place if they were givin' it away free.'

'That's what I thought. No. Dallas, you got our motives wrong. But you close up for the night and we'll talk things over in the mornin'.'

Westermann curled a lip.

'Sure – talk things over. Well, you come up with a reasonable figure and I'll meet it, Cody – providin' it's close to what Ritchie was gettin'.'

'We'll see come mornin', Dallas. Come on, gents. Move it along.'

Outside, after Westermann slammed the bars across his doors and extinguished the lamps, Cody and Starbuck, standing on the boardwalk, turned and started walking along Main.

'Think maybe we both better patrol tonight after all,' Star said and Cody readily agreed.

'Might be as well. Westermann's not the only one didn't like him bein' closed down. There's plenty of men who won't take kindly to missing out on their booze.'

'You ain't gonna win any popularity stakes.'

'So what? We won't be here long. Anyway, this is a lousy town. Needs shakin' up – might's well have a little fun while we've got the chance.'

'Uh-huh,' Starbuck agreed. 'Till they get ready to kill us.'

Cody laughed. 'You ain't gettin' nervous in your old age, are you?'

'No-oo. Just like to think I'll reach old age – wherever that is.'

'You'll know when you do – because you'll be fat and rich.'

'Mostly rich, I hope.'

They both chuckled and moved on into the deep shadows of the dark buildings lining the street.

CHAPTER 5

NIGHT PATROL

They walked side by side down several minor streets and alleys and when they came to the big side street that eventually led out to the trail to the desert, they separated.

'I'll take Main, you take Laramie. They converge just before the adobe ruins.' Cody spoke quietly, ears cocked eyes roving the shadows. He had a feeling that he didn't like.

It was a good night, stars brilliant, moon hanging midway between horizon and zenith, the town quiet – unnaturally so since he had closed up Westermann's. The two other, smaller saloons were still open but word had soon reached them about Cody coming down hard on Westermann, so things were going along smoothly.

They had rousted a few drunks and one man attempting to roll a sleeping drifter. He had got away but otherwise it had been an easy patrol.

They should have been relaxed, winding down

before going back to the law office or the hotel rooms for the night. But Cody figured this was exactly the time to sharpen the senses – especially if you had enemies who might be lurking in the night. Relax, and you could do it all the way to a marker on Boot Hill. Stay alert and . . .

'See you at the adobe,' Starbuck said, starting down Laramie Street.

Cody checked the last few stores and frame shacks at the end of Main and made his way to the adobe ruins. He settled in his usual place, one hip hitched over the edge of a crumbling wall and reached for the makings. He heard the sound – behind him – and immediately dropped tobacco sack and partly-built smoke. His hand flashed to his gun butt. On one knee, protected partly now by the broken wall, he strained to see into the shadows. The decaying walls and splintered wooden frames made strange shapes against the stars. The moonlight threw deep black pools from anything solid. His ears strained, but he didn't hear the sound again.

Might have been some animal moving away from him. Might have been. Or it could be a sound that was deliberately made so as to distract him. . . .

It was about time for Starbuck to emerge from Laramie and start towards the adobe. He should be in sight. Keeping his back against the wall, Cody turned quickly. No sign of the Indian yet. Or was that some movement over there on the weed-grown lot back of Dad Prendergast's shack. No lights in Dad's place but that was usual enough. Might be the old man making a night visit to the privy – or . . .

He was moving in an instant, heaving to his feet and starting to run. The noise he'd heard in the ruins *had* been to distract him! He saw the shadows moving over there now behind the Prendergast place – moving like two men struggling and . . .

A gun thundered behind him from the adobe and he somersaulted, twisting as he rolled up on to his shoulders and then on to one knee, now facing back towards the ruins. His right hand chopped at the hammer of his Colt and three shots shattered the night, snarling ricochets tearing across the darkness in diminishing whines, adobe dust and spraying. He saw a shadow stumble, put a fourth shot that way, and the shape disappeared.

He spun and continued his run towards the fighting men in the weeds behind Dad Prendergast's. . . .

Starbuck had felt a little disoriented as he passed around the edge of the last shack; he didn't know it was Dad's place, but that was neither here nor there. His head felt slightly muzzy and he figured maybe he should have taken Doc's advice and had an early night. That desert had taken a heap out of him and he wasn't as young as he had been in the War, when he'd led Cody's troop to safety across those badlands.

Cody had told him to cut sharp left around the sagging side fence, cross the vacant ground, and he would find himself opposite the ruins. He could see the adobe all right, thought someone was moving about over there – probably Cody.

Then he heard a kind of scraping sound that ended in a thump over in the ruins, like something knocked over accidentally – or deliberately.

Next thing he saw a dark shape leave the ruined wall, crouch low – and he knew it was Cody. He stepped forward, aiming to call out, see if everything was all right.

Then someone rose up behind him and he heard breath hissing in through clenched teeth. He whirled, caught his heel in tangled weeds and stumbled. It saved his life. He felt the burn of a razor-sharp blade slice through his shirt and open a gash across his ribs The man grunted as he stumbled against the Indian and Starbuck dropped his hand from his sixgun butt, groping for his attacker's arm, finding a bandage midway between elbow and wrist. He dug in his fingers, heard that sharp intake of breath again, wrenched, pulling the killer off balance. The man swore, a string of curses in gutter Border Spanish, and Starbuck knew who he was.

'Too eager, Spanish,' he said, moving away after pushing the man off balance.

But Spanish was quick on his feet, jumped and whirled while in mid-air, lunging back with his stiletto. He almost nailed Starbuck, ripping his shirt-sleeve and forearm. The blood flowed. The Indian grabbed at the knife arm, was cut across the hand. Spanish laughed now.

'This ain't your usual Injun knife-fight, Starbuck! Nothin' so crude. You wanna fight me, is OK. But you fight Border rules, *my* rules. Wanna get your huntin' knife out? I'll allow you that ... otherwise you're gonna die where you stand!'

Spanish was crouching, knees bent, body tensed

like a spring. Then they both jumped as Cody's gun fired in a long roar in the adobe ruins after a single shot sent a bullet whining over their heads. But they were experienced men and neither took his gaze off the other. Spanish was taunting the Indian and Starbuck, fumbling at the sheath of his knife, suddenly swore briefly.

'I prefer *my* rules, Spanish – which are no rules!' he said.

On the last word he drew and fired his Colt so fast that Spanish didn't realize what had happened when the single bullet smashed him off his feet. He flopped into the weeds, still as a statue, but bleeding from a fatal wound that had destroyed his face and distributed the back of his head in a scattering of bone splinters, hair, blood and brains, over a surprising large area of weeds.

'Star!'

Cody's call came jarring through the dark as the man ran up. But he only needed to take in the scene briefly to see that the Indian's wounds were minor – and Spanish would never bother anyone again. The sheriff stopped, already reloading his gun.

'Someone over at the adobe distracted me with some noise . . .'

Starbuck nodded, wrapping a kerchief around his bleeding forearm.

'I heard it. Spanish was waitin' for me over here, which is no surprise. You get your man?'

Cody shook his head.

'Scared him off. Heard him high-tailin' it and by then you'd nailed Spanish . . .'

'They knew just where we'd meet up, and about when. Must've been watchin' us in town while we did the patrol.'

Cody nodded. 'Yeah. Someone knew the routine. Or timed us . . .'

'Like maybe someone who used to walk the same patrol?'

Cody glanced sharply at the Indian.

'Ritchie? He quit town.'

'But could still be hangin' around out there.'

Cody said: 'Uh-huh,' holstered his gun and adjusted his hat. He looked out into the dark that Star had indicated. He nodded slowly and said, 'Oh-oh. We got visitors . . .'

After they had satisfied the curiosity of the folk who had been disturbed by the shooting, Cody and Starbuck made their way back to the hotel, started to mount the outside stairway to the second floor where their rooms were located.

They both slapped hand to gun butts as a man stepped out from the shadows under the stairs.

'Hell! Don't shoot!' the man gasped swiftly, lifting his hands to show they were empty. 'It's me – Scanlon.'

Cody lowered his gun hammer but didn't holster his weapon. Nor did Starbuck. 'What're you about?' the sheriff asked Scanlon. The man had obviously been in a fight.

'Well I – I come into town for a couple things, had a few drinks and – got into a card-game, in the back room of Dandy Grills' saloon. Lost more'n I could afford and – well, Dandy was mad when I couldn't pay. He had a right to be, mind. Anyway, coupla his men gimme a beatin' so I'd be sure to remember to pay up. I passed out. Woke up to hear shootin', seen a man runnin' by me like hell to where a coupla hosses were tethered.' He paused, straining to see Cody's face. 'It was Bill Ritchie.'

Cody and Starbuck exchanged glances.

'Figured you might like to know he's still around, Cody.'

'Yeah, obliged, Scanlon. But what the hell you still here for? I hope you ain't left young Cathy alone at your spread.' Cody took a threatening step forward but Scanlon swiftly put up his hands in front of his face.

'Hey, I wouldn't do that! My sister Rose is there.' She's been worried about me tryin' to bring up Cathy by myself after my wife died so she's come to lend a hand.'

'Good. Thanks for your news, Scanlon, but you'd better head back right now . . .'

'OK. An' you remember what I said outside the bank that day. Anythin' I can do for you, Cody, you just say the word . . .'

'Number one fan,' Starbuck opined as Scanlon went off into the night, limping a little.

'Yeah. He's all right. Little weak but he cares for his little gal, Cathy. So, Ritchie and Spanish decided to try to get rid of us, eh? Must be you, Star. I wasn't that unpopular before you arrived.'

Starbuck grunted. 'Me just dumb Injun. Wouldn't know. But me not dumb enough to pick bed closest to the window in our room tonight, paleface. That one all yours.'

Cody laughed. They continued up the shaky stairs and went in through the door at the top on the landing.

Mel Ryan banged a fist into the side of the bookcase in his parlour as he scowled at a dishevelled Bill Ritchie.

'I told you, didn't I? Said you and Spanish together couldn't take care of that damn sheriff.'

Ritchie was mighty uncomfortable.

'Mistake was tryin' to fix that Injun first. It was Spanish's idea. Said the sawbones paid more attention to Starbuck in the infirmary than he did to Spanish. He felt insulted and you know how he was when he got like that.'

Ryan sighed and nodded. He went to a chair and dropped into it. He let Ritchie stand.

'Well, you ran out again, huh?'

'No! Hell, I had 'em both shootin' at me, Mel! I traded lead with 'em but it got too hot for me to stay!'

Ryan took that with a grain or two of salt.. He tapped his fingers on the arm of the chair, looked up suddenly.

'When's Durango due?'

Ritchie shrugged, saw the cloud on the rancher's face and cleared his throat, turning his battered hat between his hands.

'Hell, he's already late after them floods up along the Cimarron. Ought to be down around Gunpowder Pass by now but no one knows for sure . . .'

'You go make sure.'

'What! All the way up there! Judas, Mel, gimme a break.'

Ryan continued as if the ex-sheriff hadn't spoken.

'Tell Durango to be mighty careful from here on in. That there's Indian trouble down this way.'

Ritchie blinked. 'I ain't heard about that!'

'Tell him there's renegades on the loose and they might hit his herds.'

'Christ, you'll send him plumb loco! You know how he hates even the smell of an Injun . . .'

Ryan merely stared back, and the suggestion of a smile moved his thin lips slightly.

'Yeah. Injun-hater from way, way back. I know Durango. His whole family was wiped out by Comanche in west Texas, years ago.'

Ritchie spread his hands, puzzled. 'Then why, Mel . . . ?'

'Because by the time he drives his herds into the holdin' pens in town, Durango's gonna be so tied in knots with hatin' Injuns that – well, sure wouldn't want to be no Injun within range, even if I *was* wearin' a deputy's star.'

At last it clicked with Ritchie. He smiled broadly, then looked puzzled again.

'But – what if Durango's herd ain't hit by Injuns?'

'Oh, it will be – Injuns, or someone who looks like Injuns. Guarantee it, Bill.'

'Helluva lot of trouble just to get rid of this Starbuck,' Ritchie opined.

'Wouldn't surprise me if Cody got in the way of some flyin' lead, too, when Durango cuts loose. Then

60

that'd leave the sheriff's job open again, wouldn't it, Bill?'

Ritchie smiled slowly, nodding his head. *Now* he savvied what Ryan was about!

CHAPTER 6

TRAIL HERD

Cody and Starbuck rode out to Pitchfork with Spanish's body draped over a stable mount. Chink Landon hadn't been too keen to supply the horse but when he saw the hardness come into Cody's face he changed his mind.

'Be thirty cents an hour,' he said spitefully.

'Charge the county,' Cody said in reply.

'Why you such a hardnose, Cody?' Chink asked, surprising himself a little. 'I stood up for you to have the sheriff's job in the first place.'

'For which I'm obliged, Chink. But you're a citizen of American River and I'm here to enforce the town ordinance. I like to do as good a job as I can. You've heard me say it before, but I can't say more'n that. Except – I don't play favourites.'

Landon still didn't seem satisfied but went about his chores while Starbuck led away the horse to the adobe ruins area where Spanish still lay among the weeds.

Dad Prendergast watched over his back fence as they wrapped the dead man in canvas and draped him over the horse, which started to shy and move away at the smell of death.

'Musta slep' through the shootin',' Dad allowed as Cody helped calm the animal and Starbuck got Spanish settled and tightened the ropes. 'But I seen Spanish and Bill Ritchie earlier on. Asked 'em where they was goin' and Spanish gimme a mouthful of that Border garbage he tosses around. Bill just told me to go back to bed.'

Cody walked over to the fence.

'They ride in together, Dad?'

Dunno about *ride* – they walked in here, damn near arm-in-arm. Had the impression Bill Ritchie was stayin' out at Pitchfork. Somethin' they said . . .' He tugged at his beard stubble, frowning hard. 'Now what was it . . . ?'

Cody and Starbuck left him to it. Far as they were concerned it was pretty certain Ritchie had been holed up at Pitchfork with Spanish.

Mel Ryan denied it as soon as he had a couple of men take Spanish away, after the lawmen's arrival.

'Dig him a grave down by the river. Ground's soft there and you won't bust your back.' Ryan turned back to the lawmen. 'Gents, I dunno where Bill Ritchie is. You're welcome to look over the place. But you won't find him here.'

'Mebbe he's out on your range – you sent him on an errand,' suggested Cody quietly.

Ryan had been staring at the silent and immobile Starbuck. Now he slid his gaze to the sheriff, shook his head slightly.

'No, both times. Anyway, what you want Ritchie for? Far as I know he quit the county.'

'He was close enough last night to take a shot at me at the adobe ruins – while Spanish was tryin' to skewer Star.'

'That a fact? Well, I know nothin' about it but, like I said . . .' He swept his arm about him. 'Go take a look around if you want.'

Cody knew he wouldn't find Ritchie here if Ryan was so ready to allow a search.

'We'll be pushin' on, Ryan. Thanks for your co-operation. But I'd appreciate it if you kept a tighter rein on your men.'

Ryan arched his eyebrows.

'Spanish? Hell, no one could throw a rein on him. Damn Mex temper. He did what he liked once his dander was up.' He looked again at Starbuck. 'Some of them men say he hated your guts, Deputy.'

'Not the first and sure won't be the last,' the Indian said easily.

Ryan's eyes narrowed. 'You speak good American.'

'Had lots of practice. Fought for the Union for four years.'

Ryan acknowledged that news with a slight inclination of his head.

'Why the Yankees? Cherokees I heard of in the war mostly helped us Rebs.'

Starbuck wasn't going to answer, but Cody spoke up.

'Star's folks had land deeded to them at the time of the treaty with Houston. Was in Carolina, up near the Tennessee line, where the Blue Ridge breaks into spurs that flank Cherokee Georgia. Finest land anywhere. Whites covet it, and the folk there couldn't stand the thought of an Injun ownin' that land. Cheated him out of it, rousted his family. So the Rebs lost a good warrior.'

Ryan's eyes slid from one man to the other; it was plain he didn't know whether to believe it or not but thought better than to say so. He just nodded, turned and began bawling orders at some cowhands working the corrals, then yelled at Red Lindeen in the blacksmith shop to get several sets of horseshoes made, adding, while looking hard at Star:

'Injuns don't bother me. Far as I'm concerned, they don't even exist.'

The lawmen took the hint and left.

'Wouldn't trust that feller far as I can throw a bull buffalo in winter coat. Which is no distance at all.'

Cody agreed with Starbuck.

'Has a tough rep around town. So's his ramrod – that was him at the forge, name of Red Lindeen. What's wrong? Name mean somethin' to you?'

Starbuck nodded slowly.

'Could be. There was a bastard of a guard at Andersonville while I was there, name of Lindeen. Had red hair, but I think they called him "Ginger". . . .'

'Got some squarin' to do?' Cody asked quietly.

'Aw, if I got the chance I'd likely lift his hair. Wouldn't waste too much time on him. But I still got a couple bones that never healed proper after he massaged 'em with his rifle butt.'

'Well, Star, I'm always learnin' somethin' new about you.'

'Only the Great Spirit knows all,' the Indian said and Cody frowned, not sure whether Starbuck was joshing or serious. . . .

Halfway back to town they saw the dust of a buckboard heading in their direction from the trail that led to the ranches. As it drew closer, they could make out two adults on the driving-seat with a child sitting between them. The man waved and the lawmen hauled rein, seeing it was Ted Scanlon.

He stopped the buckboard nearby. The other adult was a young woman, late twenties, blonde, her smooth skin reddish-tan from being newly exposed to the Western sun. Her clear green eyes looked at them candidly. Her clothes were dusted but they could see they hadn't had much use and were slightly better than the kind worn by most ladies of American River. Scanlon introduced her as his sister, Rose.

They doffed their hats and said 'howdy'. Cody winked and smiled at Cathy who gave him a shy little smile in return, but she seemed very wary of Starbuck.

'He won't hurt you, honey,' Scanlon told her with a short laugh and hugging the girl. 'He's one of the good Indians. See? He's wearin' a badge like the sheriff.'

Cathy hid her face and Rose said in a calm, easy voice:

'You are a strange sight to me, too, Mr Starbuck. If you don't mind me saying so. I mean – wearing a deputy's badge, dressed like a Westerner, complete with sixgun. I saw nothing like it in Denver.'

'Don't mind you sayin' so, ma'am. Know I'm an odd man out. Don't really care for the whites – present company excepted.' He gave a small bow towards Rose and arched one eyebrow at Cody who was scowling excessively for Cathy's amusement. The child giggled. 'Guess I like the white man's way of life better than the Indian's, though. Stores so you don't have to hunt your food, solid walls around you at night, a good sturdy roof overhead – and a soft bed to sleep in.'

Rose laughed. 'I think I agree with you – not that I've ever lived like an Indian.'

'Spoiled rotten,' Cody said. 'That's his trouble.'

Scanlon, grinning, said: 'Cody, Rose came down by stage from Colorado and she – well, you tell him, sis.'

The girl sobered now. 'Well, it's just that we passed a large trail herd out near Gunpowder Pass through the Gunbarrel Range. In fact, the stage driver argued with the trail boss, a man they called Durango, wanting him to hold back his cattle until the stage had gone through.'

Cody was interested. 'Hadn't heard about any cattle drive headin' our way. Way I understood it, the next cattle train's not due for a few weeks. If there's a herd as far south as Gunpowder Pass, why, they could be here in – well, dependin' on a lot of things, I guess, but ten days at the latest.' He hipped in the saddle to look at Starbuck. 'There's no sign of anyone gettin' the holdin'-pens ready . . .'

'Someone's an early bird – or aimin' to surprise the town,' Starbuck opined.

Rose was glancing from one man to the other.

'I – only mentioned casually that I saw the herd to my brother but he seemed as surprised as you are.'

'Well, you don't just drive a big herd in to a trail town without sendin' word on ahead – not when there're holdin'-pens to be prepared – and it's kinda early in the season, too.'

'Like I said, someone's tryin' to surprise some-one,' the Indian remarked drily.

Cody frowned at Starbuck, then nodded slowly.

'It could be us.'

'Well, we'd be as surprised as the town to see a big herd suddenly appear out on the prairie, but I don't think the surprise is aimed at any one person.'

'The whole town? queried Rose. 'But – why?'

'Think we'll have to try and find out,' Cody said. 'But I'll have to wait a few days before they cross into American River County. Jurisdiction and so on. Glad you mentioned it, Rose.'

She smiled brightly. 'I'm glad, too. I like to feel I can do something, however small, to help repay you for what you did.' Cody looked genuinely puzzled. She added: 'You saved the life of my favourite little niece!' Rose hugged the laughing child to her.

'Our whole family and kinfolk are obliged to you, Cody,' Scanlon said. 'You remember that if ever you need help.'

'I will.' Cody touched his hand to his hatbrim. As he turned his horse to ride on down the trail, Starbuck set his mount in closer to the buckboard, took somethin from his vest pocket and held it out to Cathy.

'For the prettiest little gal I've seen since my own daughter was born,' the Indian said and dropped a piece of turquoise into the tiny hand. Cathy's eyes sparkled.

'Why – it's a beautiful stone!' admired Rose. 'Thank Mr Starbuck, Cathy.'

Cathy thanked the Indian and he smiled, a genuinely warm motion that softened the leathery brown face.

'Bring you good luck, little paleface,' he said, and rode after Cody who looked at him sideways.

'I never knew you had a daughter.'

They had ridden a hundred feet before Starbuck replied.

'Not now. She died; her mother, too, when the hillbilly trash attacked our ranch. She was about Cathy's age.'

They rode on in silence and Cody thought there was indeed a lot he did not yet know about the Cherokee.

It had been a bitch of a drive so far, and didn't look like improving before they reached the holding-pens of American River. Hell, even Bill Ritchie had turned up yesterday with the news that renegade bucks were on the loose.

Durango Slade sat his horse as his men fought the last stragglers down to the rushing brown water of the river. There were three riders hazing these beasts from hell and the cows kept breaking at the last moment, slashing with their horns at the frantically dodging cow ponies.

Seven more men were trying to hold the cattle that had already crossed while three or four more riders were racing downstream along the banks, trying to keep pace with the bawling steers that had been washed away. There were at least a dozen heads bobbing about there and he glimpsed the legs of a couple more that had been turned upside down by the current, drowned by now.

Durango didn't know how many might have been lost but this time, and this time only, it really didn't matter. These cows were destined for American River and whether they all made it on to the train returning north to the meat-houses wasn't his concern. He had no financial interest in this herd: it was strictly a contract drive, set up by Mel Ryan.

Durango's job was to drive as many of the original herd as he could into the big pens at the railhead and after that – well, Ryan had some special deal going down. Durango had fallen victim to raw chance when the floods had boxed him in back beyond the ranges, and now he was behind the original schedule instead of being ahead. But it likely wouldn't matter much, because the meat train wouldn't be able to get through until the rivers went down anyway. Mel Ryan had told him just to get as many of the cows into those pens as he could by a certain date. A day either way wouldn't hurt but it would be better if Durango and his men arrived by the date set – in time to celebrate the end of the long drive.

Well, the due day was a lot closer than it should've been at this stage of the drive. But it should be easy running once they put this river behind them. Leastways that's what he'd thought. But since Ritchie's visit, talking about renegade Indians . . .

'Get that breakaway, goddamn it!' he yelled suddenly as a steer, poised on the bank to jump in after others already swimming, baulked. As it turned to plunge away the bank broke under its hoofs. There was a bellow and a great splash and then it was floundering madly, churning the river at the edge to mud.

Swearing, shaking out a loop in his lariat, Durango Slade himself rode in, roughly shouldering the cowhand aside – in fact, knocking him out of his saddle to flounder in the river, too. He dropped his loop over the steer's flailing head. Through long practice, the loop slid over the flashing horns and Durango took a fast dally round his saddle horn. Without being told the horse propped its forelegs, dug in with its hind feet, then began to back up. Slowly but surely the steer was hauled in against the sloping, though crumbling bank, and with the unrelenting tug of the rope on its neck, cloven hoofs flailed and slashed and eventually found purchase through the sludge. The horse snorted and Durango yelled as the cow found its footing and slid back on to firm ground. In a few seconds he had slipped the loop free while the animal was still shaking its head.

'Now get the son of bitch back in there and *across!*' roared Durango, coiling his muddy, slippery rope. 'Sun's goin' and anyone still workin' this side of the river come dark, stays here. No supper. I'll shoot you if you try to cross without gettin' the last of these cows over first!'

No one argued. The men were rough-tough trail hands who had been working the trails for years in most cases, and they knew Durango was tougher than all of them put together. He was a man in his fifties, grizzled, weather-burned and dried up. But his small eyes could turn mighty mean and he had no hesitation in gun-whipping a man twice his size, or even shooting him out of the saddle.

He was a man noted for delivering his herd to the contracted place – not always on time but no trail boss could guarantee that. If he saw a lone Indian on the skyline, he would spur away before a man could think of his own name. Sometimes he came back with a dripping scalp. Other times he came racing in with stone-headed arrows and hand-made bullets whining about his head as old trade rifles banged in the hands of pursuing braves.

He would gladly kill any Indian on sight and boasted he could smell one a mile off.

But it was a boast without substance – or seemed to be that night when, in the lonely, silent hours after midnight, there came an echoing war whoop and a band of shadowy riders came screaming and yelling and shooting as they swept down the slope to where the herd had bedded for the night, three miles past the flooded river.

No need to sound any kind of alarm. The trail hands were dog-tired and had fallen asleep quickly, but those blood-chilling cries woke them in an instant, groping for hats, boots and guns in that order in the age-old tradition of trail drivers in danger.

A man screamed and Durango knew it was Kid Benson, though he wasn't really a kid. He was an experienced hand of thirty-two but with a young face. No doubt destroyed now by a bullet or a swinging hatchet. Other men were raging and swearing and heavy gunshots thudded. The wrangler had his wits about him – '*Thank Christ!*' breathed Durango – and cut the picket line, herding the horses into the camp. Men bounded on to their backs – no time to saddle up – and gripping with throbbing knees and thighs, charged to meet the menace.

Already the herd was up and running. Slowly now, but it would take only minutes for it to get up speed and thunder through the night, sweeping everything before it. Something else to be thankful for was that it was stampeding *away* from the river. In fact, it almost seemed as if the attackers had deliberately cut between the herd and river to ensure it went the other way. . . .

But that was crazy and this was no time to be thinking of anything but driving off these red bastards and keeping the herd together as much as possible.

Guns were flashing and banging and lead was whining. A couple of steers had gone down, either shot or gored by the crush of their fellows, but apart from Kid Benson no one else had cried out in agony.

Durango was still trying to catch himself a horse. Most of his men were mounted. Those who weren't had dropped to their knees by their bedrolls, searching for their rifles and shooting into the darkness.

'Watch it! Watch it!' Durango Slade bawled. 'You damn fools, you'll hit our own men! Get out there so you can see who you're shootin' at!'

The men weren't keen to go anywhere on foot but started to obey when suddenly they realized that the shooting beyond the camp had died away to unhurried, isolated gunshots. Above the rumble of the herd still loping out on to the prairie, Slade heard the swift clatter of horses' hoofs and dry-mouthed, astonished, he croaked:

'They're cuttin' out! They're leavin'! Send 'em on their way!' He began firing as fast as he could into the night, wasting ammunition, but unable to stop himself when there was even the slimmest chance of one of his bullets finding a redskin target.

There was no sleep for the rest of the night but by morning they had stopped the herd, though the steers were scattered to hell and gone and they would lose another day rounding them up. But there were less than a dozen downed, mostly with broken legs, and these were swiftly dispatched, each with a bullet in the head.

Big John McKenna rode up, his horse showing a bleeding gash across the chest.

'Durango, I ain't never seen an Indian raid like that one. Hit 'n' run. Din' seem to want no cows – I mean, there's no sign of any of 'em hangin' round, waitin' till we move along and so's they can come in to butcher the downers.'

'They won't get none of my beef to fatten their verminous kids and squaws!' Durango said savagely. 'Burn every one of them downed steers! Plenty of wood so they burn away to ash! I ain't feedin' no slimy Injuns or their broods!'

Big John looked a little startled but said 'OK boss,' and started to move away. He paused. 'One other thing, Durango. None of the raiders was hit – least-ways didn't fall – but their hosses were newly shod. Clearest sign I've ever seen. Must've been brand-new shoes on them hosses they was ridin'.'

Durango frowned. 'That don't sound like Injuns,' he said slowly.

McKenna shrugged. 'Well, they either stole a bunch of hosses from some ranch – or—'

'Weren't Injuns, at all,' finished Durango very slowly – and thoughtfully.

Now what the hell? He'd thought this deal was queer right from the start but the lure of money had allowed him to accept Mel Ryan's offer without too many questions. Not that he'd have got any straight answers from Mel. . . .

But Durango was a man who rode his hunches and he was far from happy as he mounted up to go check the herd – and those tracks – for himself.

CHAPTER 7

THAT DAMN CODY

Cody couldn't rest easy now that he knew about the trail herd coming in. According to what Rose Scanlon had said, it was large enough to have blocked access to Gunpowder Pass for the stage she was on. He estimated that would mean a couple of thousand head at least.

Working steadily, he managed to get the subject into a conversation he had with Charlie Ives, the stock-agent representative of both the railroad and the meat-houses in town.

Charlie was a friendly type, liked his beer – as a chaser to whiskey – and always had a grin and a laugh ready for anyone who would stand him a drink. They were in Dandy Grills' saloon and Cody sat down at Charlie's table while the cattle agent ate his evening meal, placed a beer and whiskey beside him and lifted his own glass in salute.

'To the next season, Charlie. May it be a big one for you and a quiet one for me.'

Charlie smiled. 'I'll drink to that. Fact, I'll drink to anything!'

He laughed, ample belly jittering against the table, and Cody smiled. The sheriff toyed with his glass while Charlie smacked his lips and finished off his mangled bloody steak and fried potatoes. He belched as he dabbed his mouth with the grubby table-napkin and eased his belt a notch.

'Have to ease up on this good living, Sheriff, or I'll need a whole new set of clothes.' He laughed at his own joke and again Cody smiled.

'Town get very rough when the herds come in, Charlie?'

'Rough? Friend, you ain't seen rough until you spend a meat season in American River with herds coming in from every direction, like the spokes of a wheel. Spur track's only single line, of course, so only one train can be loaded at a time. Others have to wait on the loop out at Pinto Tanks. But you'll have several crews in town at once.' He winked heavily and nodded to the star sagging the pocket of Cody's shirt. 'You'll earn your keep then. Gonna need more'n a Cherokee Indian to keep a lid on this town.'

Cody rolled a smoke and got it going while Charlie made inroads into his drinks.

'You're one of the few folk who don't seem to mind Starbuck bein' a deputy.'

Charlie shrugged. 'When the trail herds hit, don't have time to worry about who's who or who's doing what to who, you know what I mean?'

'Reckon so. First herd due soon?'

Charlie shook his head. 'Not for a spell. Two, three

weeks, maybe. Tell you what, you don't want 'em in town too early. A paid-off crew hanging around is worse than the boys who hit us first night after the drive finishes.'

'Thanks, Charlie. Heard a rumour there might be a herd as close as Gunpowder Pass.'

Charlie straightened, smile vanishing. 'I've heard nothing. No. Too damn early. No trail boss'd want to pay holding fees waiting for the train.'

Cody left it at that. Seemed to him like Charlie Ives and the rest of the town were going to be surprised by the arrival of the herd Rose Scanlon had seen.

He couldn't shake the feeling that this was the whole idea behind the drive and if it was Durango Slade – well, he had a rep for walking a mighty slack line between good and bad. Top trail boss but never looked too closely at the brands that joined his herds, if the price was right. Maybe he would ride north a'ways and see what he could learn.

When Ritchie returned from having 'warned' Durango Slade that his herd 'could' be attacked by renegade bucks from the White Creek reservation, Mel Ryan was in a bad mood.

'The boys back yet?' Ritchie asked, referring to the men who had dressed up as 'Indians' and hit Durango's herd in a night attack.

Mel scowled as he lit a half cigar, winced at the bitterness of the first draw, and shook out the match before flicking it away.

'They're back! Two of 'em winged.'

So that was the bee in his bonnet.

'Bad enough to need a sawbones?'

Ryan's mouth hardened. 'I say 'no'. Don't care if one's gut-shot, I ain't callin' in Doc Meadows or any other sawbones.' He swore suddenly. 'Dammittohell! I warned 'em to be careful. I said just hit the edge of the herd, enough to set it runnin', put a few shots through the chuck wagon or into the camp, then hightail it outta there.' He threw up his hands. 'What does Red do? Figures to make it look "authentic", he says, so they try to set fire to some of the brush on the way out. Both men who were hit are the fools who struck vestas – made targets of themselves. Serves 'em right.'

Ritchie scratched one ear. 'Lucky they got away. If they'd been hit bad enough to fall, there'd be hell to pay from Durango, seein' white men posin' as Injuns.'

Ryan sighed, nodding. 'I know, I know. It's just that – hell, *everything*'s got just that little bit skewed lately – startin' with you showin' a yaller streak and losin' your badge to Cody!'

Ritchie flushed, 'It was Bo Bantry loused it up, Mel, you know that! He should never have tried to pull a robbery in daylight. And he sure shouldn'ta grabbed no kid hostage. He was mad with that damn Mex weed, or he'd never've done it. I figured the best thing was to just let him go and get outta town fast. So I put on an act.'

Ryan snorted and spat, ignoring the deepening colour of Ritchie's angry face.

'I *was* actin'! OK, I was scared of Bo Bantry, too! Who the hell wouldn't be when he was like that? But

I knew everythin' would blow up if I let him harm the Scanlon kid.'

'You blamed fool! Everythin' *did* blow up! You lost your law badge and that damn Cody took over!'

'Yeah, OK, OK! But wasn't no sense in me gettin' killed. I done the best I could, Mel!'

'You want a pat on the back? You messed things up. But now – now we gotta figure a whole new plan – which is why I sent the boys on that fake Injun raid to plague Durango.'

Ritchie sat down on a stump used for splitting firewood and began to make his own smoke.

'I still can't see what you had in mind.'

'Because you're dumb, Bill, that's why!' snapped the rancher, scowling at his cigar which was far too strong after having been lit for the third time. He hurled it away angrily. 'Durango hates Injuns. He was attacked by "Injuns" and there's an Injun deputy in town. *He* won't last long once Durango gets a whiff of him.'

'I know all that. We been over it. He'll come in breathin' fire and brimstone, there'll be hell raised and this Starbuck'll be lucky to survive . . .'

He stopped right there as a slow smile lifted the corners of Ryan's lips.

'Ah! If – when – Cody loses his deputy, how's he gonna police the town with a trail crew on the loose, eh? I think I see it now, Mel! He'll be too damn busy to watch anythin' else and we'll still be able to carry out the plan. Hey! I ain't sayin' I'm dumb, but I will say you're pretty damn smart! I'll even admit you're a helluva lot smarter'n me.'

Mel Ryan nodded curtly.

'There's a lot of people a helluva lot smarter'n you, Bill. I've worked too blamed long on this deal to have it go wrong now because of some Injun and a man I'm damn sure has a price on his head.'

'Too bad you can't prove it, Mel. The council'd fire him, or we could have someone kill him, claim the bounty. Either way, I'd be able to take over as sheriff again.'

Ryan said nothing, although he looked at Ritchie speculatively. Bill Ritchie was kind of pleased with himself for what he had said – but he mightn't have felt so chipper if he'd known what Ryan was thinking: *maybe he didn't need Ritchie at all now. . . .*

That would mean one whole share saved – and one share was a lot of money. A *lot* of money in this deal.

Fletcher Cody left Starbuck in charge in town – with reservations – when he started out to check on the approaching trail herd. The Indian shrugged it off; he wasn't worried about the hostility most of the town showed him. A few folk seemed easy enough about his being a deputy and that was OK by him: a bonus as far as he was concerned.

But most were leery of him now that word had gotten about how he had shot and killed Spanish; Cody had seen to it that the word spread, figuring a plus for Starbuck wouldn't go amiss. The Indian had had racial prejudice all his life, and winning a medal had done nothing to lessen it. If anything it had aroused more jealousy in whites: they hadn't liked him being able to own land that was better than theirs and had made life mighty hard for him.

It would have been easy for Starbuck to stand four-square firm and fight them off, one at a time, or *en masse*, he wasn't particular. He could have called on some of his tribe to back him, but he knew the trouble that would make – for him and every other Indian trying to escape the drudgery of reservation existence.

So he had moved on, decided to hell with owning a ranch as he had hoped to do, providing decent beef for his kinfolk and others whenever they wanted it. *That was something else that would stir up heaps of trouble with the whites. The Indian Agents wouldn't be able to run their underhand deals if someone, for once, honestly supplied the food the reservations were legally entitled to. . . .*

Then he met Cody. Both men were on the dodge, finding themselves cornered in a shale canyon with twin posses out for their blood sweeping in. Cody hadn't hesitated, had set fire to the brush, even though there was only a blind steep wall at their backs. Starbuck hadn't expected that, not a white man prepared to kill other whites in large numbers just so he could save himself.

They had escaped by hiding in a deep, sloping crevice at the very base of the cliff, hauling old dead sticks down on top of them. They had set the mounts running earlier and they, too, had made it, run off into the brush, and had been left by the posse.

Starbuck was doubled up with coughing from the smoke but Cody had wet his bandanna with the last of the water in his canteen and tied it over his nose and mouth.

'You better learn some white man ways, pronto, Star, and start carryin' a canteen. Figured you had one or I'd've shared.'

The strange thing was, Starbuck knew he wasn't just talking – he was speaking the truth. He decided then and there that here was a white man he would gladly take as a partner. They realized then that they had known each other while serving in the Union army, but, like most soldiers after the armistice, had lost touch. They hadn't recognized each other before in the heat and rush to fight off the posses.

Now Fate or something going by that name had thrown them together again – and both saw it as a sign. Both hoped it was for the better. Whether it was or not, they got themselves into – and out of – more strife than Jesse James and Quantrill's Raiders combined soon afterwards. Some of it was fun, quite a deal of it, when you got right down to things, but a lot of it was edge-of-the-knife stuff, not knowing whether a man would even see the next sunrise, nerves strung through the skin, hearts thudding hard, every sense raging and working towards survival.

And Starbuck realized this was what he had been looking for: that kind of sharp, *high* feeling he had had during the war at times of violent action: outnumbered by the Rebs or on the run with avengers at their heels, surviving cannon fire in those deadly barrages before the rebel enemy started to run short of ammunition and their guns wore out. . . .

Riding with Cody, he could duplicate that feeling and when he had it he didn't give a good goddamn in hell about whites or blacks or redmen or anything else. He was on top of the world: at those times he *lived!*

And now he and Cody were on the verge of probably the biggest and most dangerous deal yet.

And it had all come about by accident.

A month earlier a small Army detail, four armed guards and an officer carrying a locked valise, had been passing through the range folk in that part of New Mexico called the Crucibles – for the same reason that a nearby town was named Furnace Flats: it was mighty hot country.

In their travels on the edge of the law, Cody and Star had heard in three different places about this small army patrol that regularly made the run from Fort Musgrave to Fort Randolph high in the Crucibles, and back. Randolph was a kind of mystery place: no one knew much about it except that it was there to help keep control of the Indian bands that still roamed free in that part of the country. It was essentially a peace-keeping station, partly manned by hardcases from the army stockades, serving out the last of their sentences in the scorching heat of the Crucibles, under the command of a man who would have been right at home on one of the ancient Roman slave galleys . . .

So why the regular visit by a small, very small, armed patrol?

Cody learned that such patrols did actually exist.

Four armed guards and a lieutenant who carried a locked valise chained to his wrist made regular journeys to Fort Randolph about every six weeks. He figured the valise had to contain *something* of value. And when he overheard a couple of soldiers bitching about having been detailed to make such a journey to Randolph, even naming the departure time, Cody told Starbuck they would have to be plumb loco if they didn't look into it.

'Plumb loco if we do!' the Indian had retorted. 'You figure it'll be easy? When they take all that trouble? You ask me those four guards'll shoot straighter and quicker than any we've ever come up against so far.'

'So? *We* shoot straighter and quicker than anyone we've ever come against. It's gotta be worth a try, Star!'

'Another strike agin the Army, eh . . . ?'

Cody had a huge dislike for the Army. He admitted that he had enjoyed the years of fighting in the war, but it was the peacetime army that he hated. It was a long time before Starbuck learned why. Years ago, an army officer had raped and murdered Cody's wife and he had shot his way into the man's headquarters and killed him with the man's own sword. Cody had been on the run ever since, driven into outlawry – and had found that he thoroughly enjoyed that dangerous way of life.

It was the fact that he put such energy and enjoyment into their escapades that served as yet another attraction for the Indian to join up with Cody.

Cody knew those God-forsaken hills of the

Crucibles and, on one of the hottest days this side of hell, they shot a couple of the guards, left the others afoot then went after the officer who, though wounded, had escaped with his valise. But not for long.

His horse was jumped by a mountain lion and the man had gone off the edge of a cliff. He was dead when Cody and Starbuck reached him and they lost no time in cutting open the valise. There were papers inside as well as a small sack of gold money which they divided later.

They took the papers to their hideout and read them. Mostly they were boring orders about keeping control of the Indians who still wandered through the Crucibles, the need for tighter discipline among the stockade men, with orders to put them in the front line of any fighting, a cut in supplies already ordered – typical army communications.

'There's gotta be somethin' more than this to rate an armed escort and a locked valise!' Cody complained.

Starbuck had been studying some papers he had taken from a sealed envelope marked *Colonel Jacob C. Ryan, Commandant, Fort Randolph, New Mexico Territory*. He nodded a trifle absently at Cody's remarks.

'Yeah, mostly it's routine Army stuff,' he said, 'but there is somethin' else.' He proffered the folded sheet of paper to Cody who took it and, frowning, began to read, his lips moving slightly.

'Judas priest!' he breathed, looking up sharply at the Indian.

Starbuck grinned at the startled look on his pard's face – and he was a man who hardly ever smiled.

'You wanna be rich, paleface . . . ?'

'Deal me in, *amigo* – deal – me – *in*!'

CHAPTER 8

NO WIDE OPEN TOWN

Sheriff Cody was only a few miles out of town when his horse started to favour its right hind foot. He stopped and had a look, saw that the horseshoe had cracked and one part had turned slightly. He hammered the loose nail in as tight as it would go and looked around him.

A little way back he had passed a faded sign made of a splintered plank with some ranch names written on it in tar: *Pitchfork, Slash S, W – K, Lazy T* . . .

He remembered that Scanlon's place was the Slash S and only a mile or so off the trail north. So he mounted and rode easy that way, leading his limping mount in on the last few hundred yards,

Ted Scanlon was sharpening his axe at the grindstone between the corrals and a rickety iron shed which Cody figured was probably the forge and smithy. Rose was turning the handle of the grindstone while young Cathy was playing with a well-worn rag-doll in the shade of the small barn when Cody arrived. He was made welcome and when he asked could he use the smithy to make a new shoe for his mount, Scanlon led him to the rusted iron shed and helped get the forge started. Rose said she would make some coffee and went into the house, Cathy skipping along after her.

'What you doin' out this way?' Scanlon asked, working the bellows while Cody removed the broken shoe.

'Gonna check on that herd Rose mentioned.' Cody, bent over, the horse's hoof grasped between his knees, glanced up. 'Can't find anyone else in town who knows about it.'

Scanlon looked blank.

'I mean, if the stage pulled in to the depot, the other passengers and driver would have mentioned seein' Durango, wouldn't they?'

Scanlon grinned. 'Fooled you!' He gestured towards a small timbered knoll. 'Trail north is just over that ridge. The stage stopped and let Rose off and I brought her back here in the buckboard. There were no other passengers for American River so the stage just skirted the town. Saves a couple miles or more – and the stage line the cost of feedin' the passengers at a noon stopover.'

'Ah. Wondered about it . . .'

'Happens all the time with folk comin' to the ranches out this way. Stage can make the swing-station at Santa Rita by sundown then. Looks like your bronc could do with a whole new set of shoes.'

'Yeah. But ain't got time to do all four.'

'Leave him here and borrow one of my horses. I'll

shoe yours and you can pick him up on the way back.'

That suited Cody: another chance to see Rose.

He had the first new shoes roughly shaped by the time Rose called them in for coffee and fresh-baked biscuits. The sheriff complimented her on her cooking.

'I taught cooking at the ladies' college where I worked before coming out here to join Ted,' she said, smiling, noticeably pleased at Cody' remarks.

'You gave up that kind of life in Denver for this?' Cody gestured towards the window and the land beyond and saw that Scanlon looked a trifle hurt. 'Don't mean anythin' against your ranch, Ted. I just meant it's good livin' in a big place like Denver, then comin' out to the frontier . . .' He gestured again to the window. 'Well . . .'

Rose laughed 'I was born on the frontier. Our parents had a quarter-section outside Santa Fe, but we . . . lost it during the war.' She shrugged, sombre now. 'We just seemed to go our separate ways after Ma and Pa died . . .'

'You did good, sis, studyin' to be a teacher. I'm mighty obliged to you for comin' here to help with Cathy. She still misses her ma.' He went very quiet and added, 'So do I.'

Rose squeezed her brother's hand and smiled at Cody who seemed a mite uncomfortable.

'As you can see, Cody, we're a close-knit family.'

He nodded. 'Best way to be. Lost two brothers and a sister in the war. Parents had died well before that. Good for a man to have some kinfolk to visit from time to time. There's a lot of . . . comfort, reminiscin' about the early days you shared . . .'

She looked at him sharply. Here was a man she would have said was far too tough to have such feelings – but inadvertently perhaps, he had given her a glimpse of the loneliness he carried within himself – and hid so well. . . .

Yes, she thought, he was an interesting man, this Fletcher Cody. Quite interesting.

Big John McKenna rode up to where Durango was almost lost in a cloud of dust, the bawling of restless cattle making a din that mingled with the endless cursing of riders trying to haze them back into the main herd.

Durango reined up when he saw there was a rider just behind Big John. McKenna put his mount alongside the trail boss and jerked a thumb to the big man coming up to them on the dusty mount.

'Fletcher Cody, Durango. The new law at American River.'

Durango looked sharply at Cody and they shook hands perfunctorily, each man nodding jerkily.

'I've seen you somewhere. Name's not quite . . . right.' Durango squinted hard at the new arrival.

'Near enough,' Cody said, gaze steady on the trail boss's weathered, dust-caked features. 'I seem to recall you, too. Mystery Creek up in the Dakotas, wasn't it? Some . . . trouble over one of your herds . . . ?'

Durango's face straightened. 'Uh-huh. Trouble I didn't have before I bought them steers off you . . .'

'Well, things've changed, Durango,' Cody said easily. 'This time *I'm* the law.' He ran his gaze easily over the restless herd, now, at last starting to settle on the grassy flats. 'These cows look all right to me.'

Durango nodded slowly. 'They are. But I'm obliged for you sayin' so. Had our troubles on the way down, lost more'n I woulda liked to.'

'Troubles?'

'Usual stuff. Brush fire one night. Some wideloopers that we took care of ourselves, floods, even a Injun raid the other night.'

'Be interested to hear about that,' Cody said.

'Nothin' outta the ordinary, I guess. Just a hit-and-run thing. Stampeded the herd, cut away and I guess they was waitin' in the hills for us to move on so's they could come and butcher the downers.' He spat. 'But we burned 'em to ash. They never got even a cutlet – not from *my* cows.'

Cody's eyes were cold. 'Guess I can savvy how it felt, but it was kind of a mean thing to do.'

'Easy there!' said Big John McKenna suddenly, sharply thrusting his square jaw at Cody. 'That badge don't give you the right to bad-mouth Durango, mister!'

'You'd be surprised what this badge gives me the right to do, McKenna. Oh, yeah, I know you. You been Durango's dog for years – but don't go snarlin' at me.'

Durango lifted a hand as McKenna tensed, frowned, and shook his head slightly as Big John made to swing down from his horse.

'Leave it be, John. Got me a notion, Sheriff Cody's

got somethin' else to say.'

'Not much. Just that you're way early with your herd, Durango. Which means you'll have bored cowhands, likely with a part-advance of their wages, kickin' up their heels, waitin' for the meat-house train.'

'They're entitled to kick up their heels after the bitch of a trail drive we've had!'

'American River's no wide-open town, Durango. Maybe it was under Bill Ritchie, but with me it's different.'

Durango spat again and it was clear anger was shaking him, tightening his throat and slitting his eyes.

'You ain't bangin' no Bible, I hope!'

'No. But I've only one deputy and I ain't aimin' to lose a lot of sleep just because you're figurin' to turn loose your trail crew to keep 'em from gettin' bored. So, tell you what you do, Durango. You make camp out on the flats, with your herd, and let about half a dozen men in at a time. . . .'

'The hell with that!' Durango barked and Big John echoed the sentiments.

Cody looked from one man to the other.

'And they can have themselves a wingding – long as they quit town by midnight.'

The trail boss and his big sidekick were stunned.

'Reckon we're gonna have to talk about that,' Durango said slowly, and when Cody shook his head stubbornly, Big John rammed his mount suddenly into the sheriff's horse, knocking him out of the saddle.

'John!' snapped the trail boss but McKenna's well-known dander was up now and he quit leather on the run.

As Cody, a mite dazed, started to get up, Big John's boot swung into his body and sent him rolling and sprawling three yards away. This time, though hurt, Cody came up fast enough to dodge the next kick, stepped aside, and drove the heel of one hand hard into McKenna's kidneys.

The big man grunted and fell to hands and knees, aided by his own momentum. Cody gave his back two kicks for the one he had received and Big John made a sick sound as he rolled over, knees drawn up, and moved in slow motion as he started to rise. Cody let him get almost erect, set himself, and belted two lightning-fast blows into the man's face. John staggered and fought for balance and to get his guard up. Cody stepped in, swept the guard aside, hooked McKenna alongside the jaw and put him down to one knee.

McKenna shook his head, blood flying from his nostrils and smashed mouth. He started up with a roar but Cody was too fast, kicked his bent leg from under him. Big John fell heavily and Cody drove a boot against the side of his head, the man rolling on to his back, breathing like a downed buffalo.

By now, other riders had come up. Dismounted, they were cheering, yelling at McKenna to get on his feet. Durango's face was congested and he spurred his mount forward, loosed a boot from the stirrups and kicked Cody between the shoulders. The sheriff stumbled over McKenna and fell to hands and knees as the trail boss turned to his men and spoke.

'This is the sonuver who wants to turn his town into a church social while we're there! Show him it ain't to our likin', boys!'

That was all it took to raise the anger of the hard-bitten trail hands who had been looking forward to a week or so of wide-open living in American River. Cody heard and rolled swiftly, reaching for his sixgun, but it had fallen from his holster and as he lunged for where it lay in the dirt the first two trail hands reached him.

Boots thudded and stomped on his back, rough hands fisted up his shirt and hauled him upright where iron-hard fists were ready and waiting. He jolted with the blows, two men pinning his arms now. Swearing in pain and fury he wrenched and twisted as more blows landed. He kicked out, got one man where he lived and doubled him up like a folded newspaper. But any satisfaction he might have felt was soon hammered from him as men who had forsaken the herd to come and join in the beating moved in swinging.

When they were exhausted and Cody lay bloody and still in the dust, Durango spat to one side.

'Tie him to his hoss and send him on his way,' he said.

A couple of men began to look worried at the sight of the brass star dangling from the torn and blood-stained pocket but Durango seemed unperturbed. He had handled lawmen before who figured the were tough. And he knew he had a certain advantage, because these towns that depended on trail herds and their free-spending crews to make a decent living, were usually happy to turn a blind eye to many things.

If the town was wide open, everyone made more money. If damage as done to property and, often-times, to some townsfolk – well they could berate the sheriff for not doing a better job – but *after* the herd had been shipped out and the crew had moved on, to spread the word that their town was wide open and just the place to cut loose and spend freely.

'We gonna make camp out on the flats, like he wants, boss?' asked John McKenna, dabbing at his bleeding nose as he watched Cody's horse driven away with shouting and swinging hats, the battered figure sagging in the saddle.

Durango, surprisingly, grinned.

'Why not?' he said. 'Was what I was plannin' all along.'

CHAPTER 9

'HERE THEY COME!'

Cody took the glass of raw whiskey gratefully in both aching hands and nodded his thanks to Ted Scanlon. He sipped and winced as the spirit washed over the split in his lower lip. Rose Scanlon dabbed at a deep cut at the corner of his left eye, then stood back, frowning.

'I think that one needs a couple of stitches, Cody. I can't stop it bleeding.'

'I'm in your hands, Rose. Do what you think fit. And I'm sorry to bother you folk like this.'

'Hell, no bother,' Scanlon said as Rose went to fetch needle and threat. 'Glad you borrowed that mount – it brought you right home.'

Cody nodded; he, too, was grateful that the borrowed horse had brought him here, for he had been only semi-conscious most of the time on the ride back from the trail herd. Then Rose returned and Cody sucked in hissing breaths as the needle drew the tough threat through his flesh, pulling the lips of the wound together. His eye felt tight and somehow unbalanced when she was finished.

'That ought to hold, providing you don't get into any more fights.' She smiled as she gathered up the bloody rags and disinfectant and the bowl of reddish water. 'With those bruises on your body, you should rest up for a day or two.'

He shook his head and thought – for just a moment – he saw a glint of disappointment in her eye.

'Thanks all the same, but I can't leave Star alone in town any longer. He can look after himself, but – well, it doesn't feel right.'

'Of course. You'll have a meal though before you leave.' She bustled out of the room and they heard her clattering dishes in the kitchen. Scanlon looked thoughtfully at Cody but asked:

'You gonna jump Durango when he hits town?'

Cody shook his head. 'Be enough to handle as it is. I throw him in jail his crew'll tear the town apart.'

'How far out are they?'

'The flats just beyond Turkey Ridge. Take 'em a couple or three days drivin' before they reach town.'

Scanlon detected the slight edge of worry in the sheriff's words as he handed him one of his own shirts.

'Gonna be a mite lively by the sounds of things.'

'We'll see. Shirt fits OK. Obliged, Ted.'

'Come and have some grub. Your horse is all ready to go, and I can see you're itchin' to get back.'

Cody nodded but didn't say anything.

But, yeah, he was eager to get back to American

River to see how Starbuck was making out, facing the town, and all its prejudices, alone.

Starbuck had handled things pretty well, he told himself as he sat at the desk in the dim law office, oiling the shotgun he would carry on the night patrol, a box of shells beside him.

The hostility he had expected had come almost as soon as Cody had disappeared over the hogback beyond the rail siding where the train would load cattle from the pens.

He had gone into the general store and asked for a sack of Bull Durham tobacco and a packet of Wheatstraw papers. Grady, the storekeeper, face carefully blank, said they were fresh out. Star pointed to a small shelf stacked with linen tobacco sacks.

'Except for those, huh?'

'They're . . . reserved. Regular customers. Got just enough till the next shipment. Sorry.'

'How about another brand?'

The storekeeper smiled crookedly.

'Waitin' on stock. But, hey! Come to think of it, got some Injun Twist that the agent at White Creek Reservation buys sometime. Could let you have a stick or two. Know no white man would smoke it but you'd be used to it, wouldn't you?'

'Lost the taste for it long ago.' Star said amiably and walked around the counter, the storekeeper protesting, backing away, wishing he hadn't sent his helper off to lunch.

'Hey! You can't come around here!'

'One of the privileges of wearin' a law badge,

amigo. I need a smoke. Real bad. You know how it is with us smokers.'

Star reached past the now sweating storeman, grabbed a linen sack of Bull Durham and some papers and slipped them into his shirt pocket. He slapped some coins on to the counter.

'Keep any change.' he said. 'Us Injuns like to spend up big when we hit town.' He touched a hand to his hatbrim and walked out.

It was a trivial thing, Star allowed as he strolled along the boardwalk, twisting up a cigarette, but sometimes little things meant a lot more than appeared on the surface. Word would spread, probably stirring up more animosity, but maybe just a touch of respect would be mixed with it. Just a little – and that could build up, too.

Not that he would ever be truly respected but, hell, he wouldn't be here much longer anyway and he really didn't give a hoot in Hades about how the whites felt about him.

Except for Cody. There was a white man in the true sense of the word.

The saloons had tried it on that first night. Cody had been enforcing the town ordinance that said all saloons must be closed by midnight. No one ever took much notice of it but they closed when Cody had insisted. This night they must've gotten together and all three had decided to stay open.

Star visited each, gave them one warning, and one only.

'Time to close up, gents.'

Naturally, they didn't obey.

So he took his shotgun, went first to Dandy Grills' and shot out the bar mirror which was Dandy's pride and joy.

'Jesus Christ!' Dandy yelled. 'What the hell're you doin '?'

Star rammed fresh shells into the shotgun's smoking breech and aimed it at the well-stocked bar shelves.

'I'm closin' you down, Dandy. Guess you didn't hear me before.'

Grills saw where the shotgun was pointing and knew without conscious thought that he had hundreds of dollars on those shelves in bottles of spirits. As the Indian's finger tightened on the trigger, he shouted.

'*OK! OK!*' His eyes were wild as he looked around at the drinkers. 'Boys, if you want a bar to come back to tomorrow, I reckon you'd best be headin' for home.'

'Damn good advice,' Starbuck said heavily into the silence, still pointing the Greener at the shelves.

The saloon emptied, but there were plenty of savage glances – and curses – flung in the deputy's direction.

Ketchum, owner of the other small saloon in town, had gotten word about what had happened at Grills'; and was throwing out his customers when Starbuck arrived.

'You got more sense that I allowed, Ketchum,' the deputy said and the saloon man scowled.

'You ain't heard the last of this – Injun!'

'I reckon you're right.'

Dallas Westermann was waiting outside the batwings on the lantern-lit boardwalk with a crowd of men holding free drinks when Starbuck came walking down the middle of Main Street, shotgun over his shoulder.

'Just breakin' up the party, Dallas?' Star asked.

'Just gettin' started. Bar's empty. We've moved out here.' Westermann grinned tightly. 'I've closed the saloon, but nothin' in the ordinance that I know of says a man can't entertain a few friends on the boardwalk. Right, Deputy Starbuck? Or ain't you read the ordinance lately?'

'Likely can't read at all!' someone called out.

Starbuck scrubbed a hand around his smooth jaw, the Greener still angled up over his shoulder.

'Well, Dallas, you know, could be you might have me there.' The men cheered and there were several snide remarks called across to Starbuck.

'Go back to the reservation, you lousy buck!'

'How about we have a wagon race? While he's still standin' there?' That was a popular suggestion, judging by the laughter and cheers.

'Yeah. Chink's got some half-broke mustangs we could hitch up. Give 'em their heads.'

'Let 'em bolt!'

'Shoot a few holes in the sky to keep 'em runnin'!'

'Now that's goin' too far, gents,' Starbuck said suddenly, cutting short their mirth. They stared at him with naked hostility in the flickering orange light. 'No gunshots in town.' He swung down the Greener suddenly and the men stiffened as the hammers cocked and the barrels slowly travelled over the line of drinkers,. 'Unless the law does the shootin'. Anyone else and I'd have to come down real hard on 'em. Like this!'

He blasted one barrel into the edge of the walk and planks splintered. Men dived for cover. The second barrel shattered the batwings and some of the buckshot spread cracked the main window beside the door.

'You son of a bitch! exclaimed Westermann. 'Get him, boys! While his gun's empty!'

The mood was right and at least two men stepped forward, sixguns coming out of leather. Then Star discarded the Greener and his Colt bucked against his wrist in two rapid shots. One man screamed and snatched at a shattered, blood-gushing forearm, the second's left leg buckled under him and he dropped his gun as he fell writhing to the splintered board-walk.

No one else stepped out of the cowering crowd.

'Dallas, you're a hair from bein' thrown in jail for incitin' violence in the town. Get those two men down to Doc Meadows and tell him I'm sorry for sendin' him custom this late at night. Rest of you gents, well, the party's over. OK?'

No one wanted to argue about that but as the wounded men were carried away, Westermann glared at the Indian after examining the damage to his saloon.

'It ain't over for *you* yet, Starbuck. Nor Cody!'

The deputy replaced his reloaded Colt in his holster, scooped up the Greener and thrust two new shells into the beech.

'Keep an eye on the time tomorrow night, Dallas. I'll be round to check. Right on midnight. *Buenos noches.*'

Starbuck loitered long enough to see that they did disperse properly and didn't slip back again. But, no – they figured they had his measure now, he reckoned, and went their ways towards their homes or wherever they were staying.

He'd showed them how far he was prepared to go – and you could add one step more if it didn't work – and reckoned that would hold them for a while.

So he headed back on the last round before turning in, reasonably pleased with himself.

But he had made a mistake: he had made them afraid of him now.

And a man afraid was often more dangerous than a man who hated in any degree. Sometimes he figured the only sure way to get rid of his fear was to kill it at the source.

Cody's arrival back in town caused a lot of speculation as folks saw him riding slowly down Main on his newly shod horse. His injuries stood out in the hot, clear sunlight.

'Take a fall, Sheriff?' someone called.

'Looks like he took a full stampede – across the face!' another said, guffawing.

'Nah. He was always ugly as that!'

'I reckon someone beat him up. That right, Sheriff?'

Cody half-smiled. 'You oughta see the other feller. I won.'

That brought laughter from even the roughest types dawdling along the street. They watched Cody ride through the doors of the livery and a couple wandered over to see what they could pick up in the way of real news.

Chink Landon scratched at his head as Cody dismounted stiffly.

'You run into that big wildcat I hear Mel Ryan wounded the other day?'

'Just take care of the horse, Chink.'

Cody moved away, taking his rifle with him, leaving the unsaddling to Landon, who scowled.

He was watched all the way back to the law office where Starbuck, lounging in a chair and smoking, looked up casually.

'Don't say it!' Cody growled. 'I wasn't in no stampede, I didn't meet a wounded wildcat and I didn't fall off my horse.' He dropped into the chair behind the desk with a grunt and a grimace, saw Starbuck's querying look. 'I was *knocked* off my horse – by Durango. And Big John McKenna was waitin'.'

He told the rest of it and Starbuck pursed his lips thoughtfully.

'Gonna be a mighty rough old time when they hit town.' Then he went on to tell about the saloons defying him and the general animosity shown to him. 'I expected it but seemed to me like the saloon drinkers were willin' to take things a lot further. I dissuaded 'em with the Greener.'

'Well, all I can say is make sure we've got plenty of ammo and that all the guns work properly. Durango's gonna turn loose his crew no matter what.'

'He say that?'

Cody nodded. 'But I thought I'd ... dissuaded him, only without the Greener.' He touched his battered face. 'But I think this tells me he's gonna do what he wants.'

'You gonna spread the word there's a herd on the way? Spoil the surprise?'

'Might just do that. Though it's gonna make it even harder for us, the whole town on edge, gettin' ready for the first big wingding of the beef season.'

Starbuck butted his cigarette in a coffee-tin lid on the desk, which acted as an ashtray.

'Been thinkin', Cody. About why Durango was kinda sneakin' in ahead of the other herds. Can't be just to be first, 'cause often-times first don't get the best price. Meat agents know good quality beeves'll be comin' in so they hold back a little.'

'That's what's been puzzlin' me, too,' Cody admitted.

'How about if it's only to turn loose the trail crew on a certain night and tell 'em to raise hell?'

'They'll do that without the tellin' ... And what "certain nights"?'

'The night when we're s'posed to be busy. We'd have to leave what we were doin' and go take care of any big trouble in town, wouldn't we?'

Cody sat up straighter in the chair, trying to ignore the wave of pain and creaking joints it caused him.

'And leave the bank clear for ... someone who knows about the Fort Randolph shipment!'

The Indian nodded. 'Recall the name on that envelope, the commandant of the Fort?'

'Jacob C. *Ryan!*' Cody nodded. 'Yeah, I thought about those two names; wondered if Mel was somehow in on this. Now I think you've got it figured, Star! They'll be brothers or some kinda kin and though that letter said to make the shipment "*in the strictest secrecy, with all security*" Jacob could've let Mel know when to expect it.

'So. We could have competition.'

'Ye-ah! Interestin'.'

'More than that – it's gonna be downright bloody if we're right.'

Their gazes met.

'Till now, I saw that trail herd as an inconvenience, hittin' town at the wrong time far as we're concerned,' Cody said, 'but now I'm beginnin' to think it was all planned out.'

'Durango in on the whole deal, you think?'

'Mmmmm. Mebbe not. Just cash in hand for arrangin' a riot or somethin' to hold everyone's attention. Don't matter though. He's tough, old Durango, and he's money-hungry. He'll do it and with that crew he's got, he'll do it damn well!'

Starbuck rolled another cigarette and passed the new sack of Bull Durham across to Cody, who began to build a smoke thoughtfully.

'I think Bill Ritchie might be in on it. But him losin' the law job to us must have 'em worried because he'd've had ready access to the bank. No word from Meecham?'

The Indian shook his head.

'Nothin'. And there's been no soldiers in town.' He stopped speaking as they heard a slight commotion outside in the street. There was a sense of excitement, as someone shouted:

'Hey! It's the Army! A whole dang troop.'

'Ye heah! It's the soldiers! C'mon kids, come an' see.'

Cody and Starbuck hurried to the street door, the sheriff dragging slightly. They watched as a troop of soldiers rode into Main, raising dust, spurs and saddle chains clinking. The troopers were in their hot, trail-stained uniforms, a man rode alongside the officer at the head, his guidon pole-butt resting on the stirrup, the tattered, notched, half-red, half-white flag fluttering in the breeze.

In the midst of the troopers was a small army buckboard, its load covered by a tightly lashed tarpaulin.

Cody straightened and accepted the light for his new cigarette from Starbuck. He blew a plume of smoke.

'Well. Get ready, Star. Here they come.'

'I'm ready. Damn right I'm ready.'

CHAPTER 10

CLOSING IN

Mel Ryan led his men towards the dust cloud raised by the lumbering herd, told Lindeen to see the point rider about where he wanted to use the extra hands they had brought with them. Then he and Bill Ritchie rode out to the chuck wagon where Durango walked his weary mount alongside the creaking, swaying vehicle.

Behind them the wrangler brought up the remuda.

'This sure looks a tired old outfit, Durango,' Ryan said by way of greeting.

His words and the sight of the rancher brought no joy to Durango Slade's face.

'Been a hell-drive. That's why I sent Big John in to see if you could lend a few hands to help out. My men are plumb tuckered with all the trouble we've had – and we ain't gonna make it by your due date if we don't get extra help.'

'OK, OK. You've got help.' Ryan waved to his men

109

now riding with the herd. Already they were hazing the weary, uncooperative steers to more speed. 'But you're way behind. Was gonna send Ritchie out to check on you. Guess them Injuns he warned you about give you some trouble, eh?'

Durango's eyes were hard and steady as he nodded.

'Right about where he said they might . . . hit an' run. Din' make sense.'

Ryan shrugged easily. 'Who knows how Injuns think. He tell you we got one for a deputy in town now?'

Durango's shoulders stiffened like boards.

'No! How the hell that happen?'

Ryan told him briefly and Durango nodded.

'Yeah, well, I had a visit from Cody Fletcher.'

The rancher straightened in the saddle.

'Calls himself Fletcher Cody now. But I suspected it was the other way round. How the hell'd he know you were comin'?'

'Dunno. But he laid down the law about makin' it a mighty quiet time while we're in town. Wants us to camp outside on the flats, 'stead of fillin' the pens.'

Mel Ryan swore. 'Goddamn! You ain't gonna do it?'

'Figured I might. Keep the peace.'

Mel's face went red. 'You ain't bein' paid to keep the goddamn peace! You're bein' paid to raise pure unadulterated *hell*! Campin' out on the flats means you'll have to split your crew, leave half to watch the herd. I want 'em all in town, kickin' over the traces! Now you do it my way, Durango, or you'll never see

110

that five hundred.'

The trail boss's face tightened noticeably and his hands twisted his reins up till the flesh whitened.

'I made a deal – and I'll stick to it.'

'Then drive your herd into the damn pens like we agreed!'

Durango shook his head.

'Do it my way. I guarantee you'll have the hell you want – and more.' Then he smiled crookedly. 'Fact, you might even want to pay me a bonus for what I'll do.'

Ryan snorted. 'That'll be the day! Like you said, we made a deal! You stick to it to the letter or there's no money.'

He expected an explosion from Durango but this time the trail boss only smiled crookedly.

'Was gonna tell you what I had in mind, Mel, but now I won't. You can wait for the surprise, same as the rest of your stinkin' town, when I'm good an' ready.'

Ryan didn't like that and after glaring without getting any more response, he said, lamely:

'It better be as good as you say.'

'Well, I said it so you know it will be. Now let's get this herd pushed along. We oughta be there by tomorrow sundown. That soon enough?'

The rancher nodded curtly. 'Be just right. By the way, there may be some soldiers in town. Not sure how long they're stayin', but they should be good targets to get a riot started. Army and trail herders never do seem to get along.'

'Won't need 'em,' Durango said easily and spurred

111

away, calling to the wrangler to keep the horses moving.

The wrangler waved and Durango wheeled and rode out towards the distant drag-riders, Ryan watching with narrowed eyes. He didn't trust Durango – the man was a mean, greedy cuss and was likely to pull anything that suited him.

It didn't look like it when Banker Meecham came into the law office, but Cody and Starbuck had both been waiting for him to arrive.

The banker nodded curtly, turned and closed the street door.

'Kind of hot, Abe,' Cody said, winking sideways at the Indian who kept his face impassive as usual.

'Yes, I'm sorry about that, Sheriff.' Meecham took off his hat and mopped his red, sweating face with a large kerchief. ' I have to speak to you in confidence and I'd rather we didn't have to compete with the street noise – or any other interruptions.'

'Sounds serious.'

Meecham nodded, his face long with his worry, as he dropped into a chair facing the desk.

'You've seen the army troop arriving, I'm sure.'

There was nothing to say to that and the banker didn't pause long enough for a reply, anyway.

'Special detail from Fort Randolph. You noticed the buckboard, covered with a tarp? Of course you did.' He paused and hitched his chair a little closer, flicking his gaze from one lawman to the other. He lowered his voice as he said: 'It was carrying a pay chest . . .'

He obviously expected some surprise from the lawmen but they merely stared back, waiting. Meecham licked his lips.

'It has to stay in the bank safe and be shipped out on the meat train to Fort Worth.'

Now Cody dropped in a question.

'Seems a long-handled way of goin' about it, don't it? And how come Randolph of all places sends down the money?'

Meecham smiled crookedly. 'You must've heard about all the hold-ups around the mountains? Banks, stages, one train, two or three army pay details . . . ? Yes, I thought you had. Been going on for weeks and no one seems to be able to find out who's doing it, let alone track them down to their hideaway.'

'Must be some tracks,' opined Starbuck and Meecham shifted his gaze and shook his head.

'Not according to the army. I mean, there may be tracks but they peter out, become lost in wild country, never seem to lead anywhere.'

'Probably headed into Badman's Territory,' allowed Cody slowly. 'Fort Randolph'd be the closest out there. Haven't they come up with anything?'

'Apparently not. They're not . . . the best of soldiers up there, you know.' Again the banker lowered his voice. 'Not many know it, but they send a lot of the army stockade prisoners to Randolph to finish their sentences. It's a very bleak and primitive place, very, very strict, and run by a hard commandant. They may think they're going to have a measure of freedom but once there under harsh discipline – well, in those hills where can they possibly go, even if they do attempt to run?'

'Indians still live there. Years ago they hit the white settlements, afterwards losin' themselves in those hills,' Starbuck said quietly.

'Sounds a lot like what's happenin' now with all these raids, 'Cody said quietly.

'Well, the Indians are suspect, of course, but while they are still troublesome it's not likely they would just steal money. They'd be more interested in trade goods or ammunition and guns. White outlaw gangs are the real suspects. Anyway, as I was saying, because of all these hold-ups in that area, the commandant at Randolph, a Colonel Ryan – brother of Mel Ryan, I understand – suggested that when it came time for the next big payroll, why not ship it to Randolph over the range, a little at a time, hidden amongst supplies in the pack mule-trains? And once it was all there, it could be sent on to Fort Worth down a safer route through American River, this town having the bank with the most secure facilities? My – *our* bank, the American River National! It's a real honour to be chosen, gentlemen . . .'

Meecham paused, awaiting a reaction, and Cody and Starbuck exchanged a glance. *So that was how they were working it.*

They had wondered ever since reading that confidential letter they had found on the dead messenger. *Why would isolated Fort Randolph be chosen to send a large army payroll through American River?* Now they had the answer.

'How much is the payroll?' Cody asked casually. It had said no more than a payroll of 'substantial proportions' in the letter.

Meecham looked uneasy.

'I'm not supposed to tell anyone – but seeing as you gentlemen will be guarding it – I did mention that, didn't I?'

'Not till just now, Abel,' Cody said slowly.

'Well, it's why I came to see you. The army want the local lawmen to guard the safe as long as the money's in it. I thought you might work it between you. I'd prefer that you didn't hire any extra help.'

'We can work that out, Abe, but how much is it, for God's sake?'

Meecham drew in a deep breath.

'You see, it's not just for disposition at Fort Worth. That being a more or less central location for other army stations in that part of Texas, it's been chosen as the distribution point and—'

'*Abe!*' Cody said sharply and Meecham jumped.

'I know. I'm sorry. It's just that I'm still reluctant to go against the army's request not to tell *anyone...*'

When he saw Cody moving restlessly and the sheriff's tightened lips, the banker hurriedly said: 'Twenty-seven thousand dollars – and some odd hundreds.'

Cody whistled. Starbuck's face showed nothing: no excitement, not even interest. 'It's a six month's allotment for several forts, you see . . .'

'OK, Abe. We got it now. I tell you, I'm not too keen to take on the responsibility. Can't the army troop stay and lend a hand?'

'No. That is, not *en masse*. If absolutely necessary they may be able to spare a man, but their orders are to deliver the cash-box to my bank and then head north-east to follow up reports of a recent uprising of Comanche in the Territory. Several whites are said to have been butchered.'

'Settlers?'

'Er – well, I should think so. I'm sure the US Army wouldn't send soldiers if the Indians only slaughtered outlaws hiding out there.'

Cody nodded. 'What d'you say, Star? Big responsibility guardin' all that money.'

'Well, I like to think I've got this town quietened down some. I reckon we could handle it between us.'

Cody nodded. 'Yeah, I guess so. All right, Abel. When d'you want us to get this organized?'

'Why, right away. For tonight, certainly, but if one of you could stay close to the bank during the day, make regular checks, you know . . . ?'

'Gonna stretch us some. We can't work all day and then stand guard all night. Might have to adjust our pay.'

Cody arched his eyebrows at the banker, saw the instinctive tightening of the mouth at mention of spending any amount of money, and then Meecham nodded.

'All right. I – I have to keep this secret even from the council, so I'll see if bank funds will run to an increase for you, Cody.'

'For both of us.'

'Oh. Yes, of course, I meant both of you.'

Cody knew he hadn't, but he didn't press the point; it was enough to have asked for 'danger money'. It might raise a few suspicions if it got around that he and Star were going to be working their butts off without at least asking for some cash compensation.

For he knew Meecham would never be able to keep this to himself. Hell, the man was almost busting with pride right now, pride that 'his' bank had been chosen for the responsibility of holding so much cash. He'd at least tell his family, and then Mrs Meecham, second biggest gossip in town after Chink Landon, would do the rest. . . .

Meecham didn't realize that the Ryan brothers had earmarked the American River National for the keeping of this payroll long ago: it was no snap decision.

They must have been worried when Bo Bantry and his bunch hit the bank and had almost gotten away with robbing it. Something like that, pointing up the vulnerability of the bank, could have made the army change its mind about where to leave the payroll 'resting' until the meat train, no doubt specially rigged out with armoured caboose, could convey it to Fort Worth.

Someone had worked hard and fast to convince the army that all would be well. And probably it would have been – except that Cody had intervened and the town in its excitement and gratitude had made him the law at American River, even if they did regret it now. It must've made Mel Ryan spit blood, losing his man Ritchie at such a time.

'Still, at least three days till the train arrives, Cody.' Starbuck said after the sweating banker had left and Cody had propped the street door open to let in some fresh, though dusty, air. 'When we gonna get rich?'

'Give Durango another day to get here. I'll stir him up again by tellin' him we want a quiet town while his men are here. That'll guarantee that he'll turn 'em loose to raise pure hell and keep the town's attention focused on 'em. And that's when we retire . . .'

Starbuck grunted. 'After we cross Satan's Platter – don't forget that little detail.'

Cody grinned. 'They won't even look for us there. They'll figure we'll make a run for Indian Territory where all the outlaws hole up. Anyway, *amigo*, got lots of faith in you, lots and lots.'

But someone threw a spanner in the works and Cody's and Starbuck's plans for big, easy money seemed to dissolve into the stuff of dreams.

Starbuck, never a popular choice as deputy, had now earned the utter hatred of the saloon-owners. Other businessmen who had had their hours curtailed by the Indian said aloud that they hated his guts, but did nothing more about it.

Not so Dallas Westermann, Dandy Grills and Ketchum, the three saloon-owners, all of whom ran a profitable business in prostitution on the side. They were about to lose a lot of money, *heaps* of money, if the town ordinance was enforced as Starbuck threatened. The trail-driving season was their busiest and most profitable time and they needed a wide-open town to take maximum advantage of it. And an early start would suit them fine.

If Starbuck and Cody figured to cut into those profits by sticking to the letter of the law, then something had to be done about it. And, as they had all tangled most recently with Starbuck, plus the fact he was a full-blood Indian, they reckoned to vent their spleens on the Cherokee.

They hired Red Lindeen, a man who had killed before in drunken brawls and who was barely restrained by Mel Ryan – in fact, at times turned loose when Ryan didn't get his own way. And Red had little love for Indians; one had tried to scalp him a few years back. Red was always looking for a fast and easy dollar. A few double-eagles would buy his gun.

'You gotta make damn sure – *damn* sure, Red, that it can never be traced back to us,' Westermann told him edgily.

'Relax. Nothin'll go wrong. The day I can't outfox some lousy Injun you can dig me a hole on Boot Hill and drop me in without so much as a coffin,' Red told them, jangling the golden coins in his pocket. 'Tonight be all right?'

'Tonight will be perfect,' growled Dandy Grills. 'Only wish I could be there to see it.'

'You'll see him in Doc Meadows' mortuary,' Red told them confidently. 'Thanks for the business, gents. Oh, I'll expect a few free drinks in your bars afterwards – OK?'

They nodded but didn't like him holding them up for even that much beyond the original deal.

'And mebbe a little pleasure time with some of your gals?' Lindeen pushed.

'Do the job first and we'll talk about it, Red,' Ketchum grated.

'Sure,' Red Lindeen said as he left the darkened room at the back of Westermann's saloon, swaggering. He knew he'd get his extra demands – they couldn't risk not keeping him happy.

The soldiers stayed overnight, so it was a pretty noisy town after dark. Cody and Starbuck divided their patrol areas, showing their badges at the three raucous saloons, reminding the owners that there was a midnight close-down. There were complaints, of course, but none of the three seemed to press for longer hours as Cody had expected.

Frowning, he paused to roll and light a cigarette outside the general store, lifting a boot to the hitch rail beyond the edge of the raised boardwalk, thinking about the reactions of Westermann, Ketchum and Grills.

He had figured there would be more voluble complaints, maybe even threats – or, possibly, the offer of a bribe. But there had been nothing, only sour acceptance, which he couldn't quite swallow. Not from those three. . . .

'Now why in hell would they act that way?' he murmured to himself.

An instant later, he felt his blood turn cold as he heard three gunshots two blocks away.

'God almighty!' he said aloud, flinging away his cigarette and starting to run towards the sounds of gunfire. 'There's the answer!'

And when he skidded into an alley where he

smelled gunsmoke and saw the sprawled dark body with the glistening trickle of blood snaking from beneath it, he knew someone had finally settled their fancied grievance with Starbuck.

And saddled *him* with one hell of a problem: How was he going to watch the town, guard the safe – and still get his hands on that payroll now?

CHAPTER 11

LONER

Just as he heard running footsteps behind some of the nearby buildings, men came crowding into the alley wanting to know what had happened.

Cody wanted to get after whoever he had heard running off – but he also wanted to check on Starbuck. Swiftly, he knelt beside the Indian, placed two fingers on the side of the brown neck. A pulse still beat there, erratic and weaker than it should have been, but it was beating.

He looked up at the gathered men in the bad light, heard a couple of remarks:

'Someone finally got that Injun!'

'Hell, is that all? I left a full glass on the bar for that?' There was a spitting sound and a few men moved out of the alley, muttering.

Cody stood and grabbed the nearest townsman.

'He's still alive. Get him down to Doc Meadows, pronto.' They saw his eyes glittering darkly in the light reflected from Main. 'And he better get there quick because I'll check when I get back. On you, Handy, you, too, Aaron Case . . .' He swept his hard gaze around the dimly seen faces. 'I'll remember who I saw here. *Now get movin'!*'

Then he was running down the alley to where it turned behind the buildings fronting Main, sixgun in hand. He paused, listening, before his hearing was impaired by heavy and ragged breathing from running. *Yes!* Over there to the right and out towards the clump of trees that lined the small creek which ran through this part of town. A good place to leave a get away mount.

Cody started running again, sticking to the long grass where the tangle of weeds would muffle his jarring boots. But there were obstacles hidden by those same heavy pads of weed: rotting boxes, discarded bottles that could turn a man's foot under him, bits of rusting machinery, stumps and roots. He fell twice, the last time his gun skidding from his grip. On hands and knees he searched frantically for it. Two shots tore at the night and he reared back as a bullet clanged against something only inches from his right knee. Then his groping hand closed over his Colt and he fired a wild shot, making the killer keep his head down long enough for him to leap to his feet.

Cody was up instantly, launched himself bodily for the protection of an overturned rain-butt with sagging staves. The killer had sharp eyes, for his next shot shattered one of the staves and the following one *whanged* and ricocheted from a buckled iron clamp-ring.

The sheriff saw where the man was now, across the creek – wading over had slowed his escape some. He saw the moving shadows as the man tried to mount his skittish horse. Cody knelt, steadying his aim by wrapping his left hand around his gun hand, pulling back while he pushed with his right. He drew his bead, and fired as the killer lifted towards his saddle. There was a grunt that almost, but not quite blotted out the sound of lead slapping against flesh and then the horse whinnied and the wounded man flung himself across the saddle, hanging on as the mount ran into the timber.

Cody fired again, heard his lead *thunk!* into a tree. Then he ran for the creek, ducked instinctively as a gun hammered, but he didn't even hear where the bullets went. The man was hit, but not badly enough to stop him returning fire apparently.

Cody skidded on the bank and, as he tried to stop his forward momentum, slipped over the edge and floundered in the creek. By the time he'd straightened, groped for his gun underwater, he knew the killer had made good his escape.

Swearing, he sloshed and squelched his way back to town. It would be useless trying to track the assassin in the dark. But he would be in the saddle by sun-up, looking for blood-spots and fresh tracks.

He would get the son of a bitch: there was nothing more certain. Meanwhile, he made his way towards Doc Meadows'.

'I – I think he'll pull through, Cody,' the sawbones said slowly, 'but I can't guarantee it Two bullets in him.

One in the back, which, unfortunately, I fear has grazed a lung, and the other alongside the head, just above the left ear. In fact, it took a piece of the ear with it and that was where most of the blood came from.'

'Likely saved his life,' Cody said, grim-faced, looking down at the greyish face of Starbuck in the bed, head and chest swathed in bandages. 'When the killer saw all that blood he must've figured he'd killed him and ran for it.'

Doc Meadows stifled a yawn.

'I could wish you and your deputy would keep better hours, Cody.'

The sheriff smiled crookedly.

'Figured you'd appreciate the custom, Doc. I'll sit here a spell before I go back to finish patrol. Then I'm s'posed to get on down to the bank.'

Meadows blinked. 'This time of night? Oh, I see. I'm not supposed to ask. Well, move your chair over into that corner. I'll bunk down outside and if you're not in the way, I'll be able to see Starbuck's bed from my own.'

Cody moved his chair into a corner beside a narrow cupboard, adjusted position and tilted it back so that his shoulders rested against the angle of the walls. Despite himself he closed his eyes, listening to the heavy, crackly breathing of Starbuck and soon drifted into sleep.

But it was a shallow sleep. For years, even before the war, he had slept lightly and it had saved his neck on more than one occasion when a night posse was creeping up on the hideout, hoping to take his wild bunch unawares.

Tonight, it worked once more.

A shadow flitted across his face and his eyes opened instantly, his brain trying to catch up with the warning signals that flashed through his nervous system. He didn't move his body, but his eyes rolled in their sockets – towards the window at the end of the room and which he could see clearly from his darkened corner.

The blurred outline of a man showed against the smeared glass and then he heard the low screech of wood as something was jammed under the frame, strained briefly, then lifted. Grasping fingers worked their way under the frame and eased it up high enough for a leg to thrust into the room. The shadow bent and the man's upper body straightened slowly. Cody saw the glint of light on gun metal.

An instant later he heard the ratchet of a hammer cocking.

Cody let the chair legs drop to the floor as he came out of it on the opposite side of the bed to the intruder, palming up his sixgun. The man heard him and swung his gun in his direction and both Colts roared simultaneously, the muzzle flashes briefly lighting the room, showing the wounded man on the bed, the crouched lawman – and the killer driven back by the strike of lead. The man's arm jerked up and backwards, his gun shattering the glass of the lower panel before he spilled out into the night.

Cody was across the floor in an instant, vaguely aware of Doc Meadows shouting in alarm from the room next door. The sheriff slammed into the wall, sidled along it, Colt raised, hammer spur under his thumb, trigger depressed But he only had to look once through the broken window to see that the would-be killer wouldn't be escaping into the night this time.

Abel Meecham was very nervous when he met Cody outside the bank and let him inside.

'We – heard all that – shooting . . .'

'Someone tried to kill Star. Red Lindeen.'

'Good lord! Is – Mr Starbuck all right?'

'No, he's lung-shot and head-shot.'

'I'm sorry to hear that. Lindeen is – in custody?'

'The devil's custody. I was waiting for him in Star's room. You'd best leave the keys with me, banker.'

Meecham stiffened. 'What! I can't do that!'

Cody looked at the man in the dim passage just inside the rear door of the bank which now stood partly open.

'Look, I'm to watch the safe, all right? OK, but I hear a riot or somethin' in town, I have to go check on it. Don't gimme an argument, banker! I told you it could happen, but when Star was to work nightshift with me we could've managed it between us. Now I'm by myself, I have to do both jobs. And it's no use if I can't get out to go stop a riot, and lock the bank after me.'

Meecham saw the sense in that but was far from happy, although he could see that Cody had no choice.

'Look – I'll give you a key to this door only, all right? But you have to get it back to me as early as possible in the morning. I'm not supposed to let it out of my keeping.'

Cody had hoped the man might hand over the ring of keys for the night. It would save a lot of trouble when it came time to get the payroll out of the safe.

Now he would have to make other plans. Of course, he'd have had to make them, anyway, with Star dying. No use fooling himself: the Indian was hit pretty bad.

He held out his hand, felt the cold metal of the door-key against his palm and then ushered the banker out, locking the door after him.

When he saw the safe, he knew he was in real trouble. It was more like a vault, bolted to the floor, seven feet high, big enough to allow a man to walk inside. There were two separate keyholes and what looked like one of those new-fangled combination locks that could only be opened by someone who knew the right numbers.

The massive door must be inches thick.

No wonder the army were happy enough to lock their payroll up in this monster. It would take a cannon or a full case of dynamite – maybe both – to blow it open.

All he had was his bare hands and what passed for intelligence.

Somehow, he didn't much care for his chances of success.

CHAPTER 12

HELLTOWN

Starbuck was a little better when Cody went to see him next morning. The man was conscious but obviously in a great deal of pain. He coughed frequently into a soiled rag.

'You – gonna have to – do it – alone, paleface,' he said haltingly in a harsh whisper as Cody sat beside his bed.

'Alone? Hell, we need the old gang and a case of dynamite – and even that mightn't do it.' He lowered his voice although there was no sign of the doctor right now. 'Looks like there could be a combination lock.'

He wasn't sure that Starbuck had heard, for the man said nothing and his eyes remained closed. Then, a hoarse whisper:

'Make – Meecham open it.'

Cody looked at him sharply.

'That's the very thing we didn't want to have to do, Star – involve the banker!'

'If it's – tough as you – say – got no – choice. Get – Meecham to open the safe.'

The sheriff wasn't happy even thinking about it.

'We blow our chance of at least some kind of a lead if we do that.'

'Tie him up, gag him. There's no – choice, Cody. I can't do – anything.'

'That's the other thing, Star. Doc says you're improvin' but won't be outta here under a month.'

Star made a brief snorting sound.

'He – dunno how tough an Injun can – be. Yeah, I'll be laid up a spell, but you go ahead. I'll catch up with you – sometime.'

It had been nagging at Cody all night and ever since he had woken this morning: *what was he to do about Starbuck?* The whole thing had been planned for them both to rob the safe, then make their getaway across Satan's Platter, the last place anyone would expect them to go. No one knew for sure how many had perished out there in that white, blazing hell. But Star had made it across one corner and figured he could find a way back through the alkali. Still, there were no maps, no real instructions he could pass on to Cody. It was *instinct*, pure and simple. *Indian* instinct, bred into him through long-dead ancestors. He could find a way because he would call upon these 'spirits' when he needed them, he said. Cody was sceptical but had seen Star do some near-wondrous things in the past and had been willing to take his chances with his pard. But now . . .

'The plan's shot, Star. I hate to pass up that much

dinero, but I can't see any way of my doin' it alone.'

'*Do it!*' Star grated. 'You can. Cut corners – ride south-west to the hills. Then go due south to El Paso. You can make it that far. Cross the Rio to – Juárez.'

'Judas priest! Is *that* all. What do I do, fly?'

'You'll – make it.'

Cody was still doubtful but admitted privately there might be a chance going that way; the posse would be relentless, specially if Ryan was there with his men – and he would be. He had a vested interest in that payroll.

'I can't leave you, Star.'

'Damn fool white man! *Gotta* leave me. I'll turn up. Have to. I wanna be rich, too – remember?'

Cody left, the whole thing weighing heavily on his mind. Then he received another jolt. A rider was coming in fast, dodging through the traffic on Main, almost colliding with a wagon team. He hauled back on his reins so hard he pulled his sweating mount up on to its hind legs. The wagon driver cussed him and someone on the boardwalk called out.

'What in hell's wrong, Buddy? Injuns comin' . . . ?'

The sweating, dust-spattered rider fought his horse down and swivelled in the saddle to yell:

'Hell no, Briscoe. I just seen the first trail herd edgin' through the pass. Must be a coupla thousand head. It's early but means she's gonna be a high ol' time in the ol' town tonight!'

Men crowded out into the street for more details, hemming in the rider. Cody stopped in his tracks. *Damn Durango! The man had made much better time than he'd figured!* He would be here before sundown and

131

that meant he would turn the trail crew loose as soon as the herd was bedded down. Like Buddy Doran had just said, it would be a high old time in American River tonight. And *he* had to try to keep control.

And figure out a way to get his hands on that payroll in the bank. Maybe he'd have to leave it till later.

Then, just to make his day, Mel Ryan came riding in with a dozen of his cowhands, and he could see they were more than ready to cut loose the curly wolf. So it would have to be tonight! Ryan wasn't here just for the fun, even if his men were. Cody strolled over as Ryan and his crew dismounted.

'Come lookin' for Red Lindeen?' Cody asked and Ryan started at him coolly, Bill Ritchie at his side.

'Now why would I be lookin' for Red?'

'Dunno, but if you want him, check at the morgue.'

Both men stiffened and the cowboys within earshot looked sharply at Cody.

'What happened?' Ryan asked.

'He tried to kill Starbuck – damn near succeeded.'

'Hell, I know nothin' about that!'

Strange thing was, Cody believed Ryan. The rancher's reaction was genuine and Ritchie and the cowhands sure seemed surprised. Cody started off and threw over his shoulder;

'Keep a rein on your men, Ryan. I'm busy enough without your crew kickin' up their heels.'

Ryan scowled. 'Wait till Durango gets here!'

Ritchie and the cowboys laughed and whooped.

Cody spent the afternoon cleaning and oiling all

the weapons available to him, both his personal guns and those belonging to the law office. He checked on the saloons and the owners seemed pretty damn smug, Westermann going so far as to ask: 'How's that Injun? Hear someone tried to kill him.'

The man could barely keep a straight face and Cody knew damn well this son of a bitch had likely hired Lindeen. He kept a hold on his rising anger, checked the other saloons and got the same kind of treatment, convincing him that it had been the saloon men who had tried to have Starbuck killed.

Ryan's crew were rowdy and getting drunk fast enough but their behaviour was no more than would be expected of a bunch of cowhands in for a spree, with money in their pockets.

But mid-afternoon, Durango's herd arrived and you could *feel* the difference in the town's mood. Prices went up within minutes of word reaching Main that the herd was on the way. Price placards, still wet with the ink, were changed swiftly in display windows of stores and the barber's shop, even the druggist's. The livery, too, doubled its prices and rooming-houses pushed their rates up as if they were trying to make their fortunes overnight.

Trail hands with full pockets paid no attention; they were here to have *fun* and to raise a little hell. No point in arriving in a town that was all ready to fleece them without giving the folk who were doing it something to remember them by.

After breaking up a couple of fights, Cody rode out to the river flats where Durango and his men were bedding down the herd. Big John McKenna saw him and, scowling, nudged Durango. The trail boss leaned back against a lodgepole pine, reaching for his pipe and tobacco pouch.

'This all right, Sheriff?' Durango asked civilly.

Cody folded his hands on the saddlehorn.

'Glad to see you co-operatin'.'

'We-ell – we were kinda rough on you.' Durango looked up as he jammed his pipe-stem. between his teeth.

'We've had our misunderstandin', Durango. If you're smart, you'll make sure there's not another.'

Durango puffed hard to get the tobacco in his pipe-bowl going.

'Hell, I ain't worried – one way or t'other.' He to McKenna. 'You worried, Big John?'

'When someone like Cody makes *me* worry, you can light the lamp – because that day the sun won't rise!' Big John touched a hand to his battered face, looking mean and nasty.

Cody smiled thinly. 'I almost believe you, John.'

'I said it and I mean it. You don't bother me none.'

'Shows you ain't as smart as you think you are. Just keep your men from wreckin' too many bars, Durango, then you an' me'll get along.'

He turned and rode back towards town. Big John spat then grinned tightly.

'Now ain't *he* in for a surprise.'

Cody went to see Star again after supper.

'You gotta do it tonight,' the Indian said. 'The trail men'll be a good diversion.'

'Maybe. Folk'll expect me to try and cool 'em off.'

'Best time to get the loot, paleface.' Star's voice sounded weak and he coughed a lot. 'Hit an' run while Durango's tearin' up the town, got folks' attention.'

'I don't want to have to slug Meecham: he's too old.'

They didn't argue about it. Then there were a couple of gunshots and the sounds of breaking glass. Cody sighed, and stood up.

'Better go show the badge.'

'Luck, Cody,' Starbuck said, lifting one hand in a weak salute, a gesture of farewell.

Somehow it looked kind of final to the sheriff.

Cody had a bite to eat in a café just before sundown and he could feel and hear the increased celebrations of the trail crew and Ryan's men. There was a lot of hard joking and fun-poking that could easily be taken for insult – and would be when a few more drinks had been put away.

He was leaving the diner, rifle swinging in his left hand, when he almost collided with a man about to enter. Cody raised his eyebrows in surprise, recognizing Ted Scanlon.

'Didn't expect to see you in here, Ted.'

'Come lookin' for you. Heard about Star and figured you might need a deputy.' The young rancher cocked his head towards the nearest saloon where shouting told them another fight had broken out. In the distance, they could hear the bellowing of restless cattle.

Cody was surprised by Scanlon's offer.

'That's right thoughtful of you, Ted, but I'll manage OK.'

'Hell, I ain't had the ride for nothin', have I? C'mon, Cody, you can't do this by yourself – tryin' to watch the town and the wild bunch that's here tonight – and keep an eye on that payroll as well.' Scanlon laughed at the way Cody looked. 'Hell, man, it's all over the county. Everyone an' his brother knows Meecham's spendin' most of his time in the outhouse with the Fort Randolph payroll sittin' in his vaults!'

Cody sighed and smiled crookedly.

'I ought to've guessed – a town like this. I don't want you involved, Ted, but much obliged for the thought. I'll buy you a drink before you ride back to Rose and Cathy.

Scanlon stayed put as Cody went to take his arm. He spoke quietly.

'I've been to see Star.' There was something in his voice that made Cody tense. 'He's worried. Not so much about you takin' on the town alone, but doin' that other job without help.'

Cody said warily: 'Thought I'd convinced Star I could manage watchin' both the bank and the town . . .'

Scanlon smiled thinly, took something from his jacket pocket. Cody was surprised to see a small can with a conical top, a cork protruding. He smelled something kind of sweet.

'What's that?'

'Somethin' Star slipped me – chloroform.' He studied Cody closely, saw the sheriff frown.

'That's knock-out stuff, ain't it?'

Scanlon nodded slowly. 'Star said you might find a use for it – when you're on bank duty.'

'Must be ravin' . . .'

'Uh-uh – he's lucid enough. Said no one'll get hurt if you use this stuff.' He shook the can.

Cody took it, felt the ice-cold metal. There was no label but 'Chloroform' had been stamped on the can from the inside in raised letters. He knew Star had sent this to use on Meecham – instead of knocking the banker out with a gun butt. He slipped it into his pocket.

'Not my business, Cody, but I can put two and two together. Someone's gonna go to sleep mighty sudden and I think it's Abe Meecham – after he opens the safe.' Cody still said nothing, not liking this, but Scanlon held up a hand. 'Stay calm. Like I said, nothin' to do with me. And just for the record, I ain't had any experiences with this US Army that I'd want to remember to tell my grandkids . . . So what happens to one of their payrolls don't bother me at all.'

'I dunno what you're talkin' about, Ted.'

Scanlon grinned, shaking his head.

'You know I catch my own broncs. Well, I've got me some good ones right now, fast, plenty of stamina. They'd take a man to hell and back.,'

Cody was silent and Scanlon waited him out.

'Well, Satan's Platter is a part of hell, I guess, Ted, but I was only countin' on makin' a one-way passage.'

'That's what I figured. Well, my broncs'll do it with their ears laid back. You won't let me help you in town, so let me help on your way . . . out.'

'How much did Star tell you?'

'Nothin'. Just gave me the chloroform. Look, Cody, Cathy owes you her life. You *have* to let me help, man!'

'I don't want to involve you, Ted. But . . .' Scanlon's face lit up expectantly. Cody sighed. 'I'm desperate. Leavin' Star bothers me. You do this and I'll cut you in—'

'No you won't! What you're plannin' don't mean nothin' to me. I just want to help you get away safely. That's reward enough. I'll even lay a false trail away from my spread. And if Star pulls through and needs nursin', why Rose'll be happy to do it.'

The sheriff still wasn't sure about this, but it would be a mighty fine thing to be able to change his mount for fresh, young, strong horses and know that Star would be in good hands.

'You tell the posse I held you up for the broncs. Make out you're another victim.'

'Don't worry about my end. Look, if you *do* need a hand in here with whatever you're plannin'—'

'No, Ted. You'll be doin' enough.' There came a roar from the saloon, a crash and more shouting. 'Things're hotting up. You head on back to your spread. And *muchas gracias, amigo.*'

They shook hands and parted, Cody starting to run when a gun banged in the saloon, followed by a heavy silence. . . .

Full darkness brought more trouble than Cody could reasonably be expected to handle alone. Brawls, one gunfight with a trail hand being shot in the foot. Cody bent a gun barrel over his opponent's head, toted him to jail and threw him in a cell. Within an hour, the man had four companions; two trail hands, one of Ryan's crew and a sick-and-sorry townsman.

Cody took a lot of abuse for locking them up until he went back and got the Greener and showed it around. Things actually quietened down for a while then and he was in Westermann's saloon bar when a man came in and told him that Banker Meecham wanted to see him right away. Westermann was trundling in yet another keg of beer. He looked up and said with a leer:

'Bet you could sure use that Injun right now – if he weren't dyin' at Doc Meadows'.' The man could barely keep a straight face and Cody *knew* then, for sure, that Westermann had been involved in the assassination attempt on Starbuck. He brought up the shotgun's butt and smashed it into the middle of the saloon man's face, turned and went out, leaving the suddenly silent crowd gaping at the bloody man writhing on the floor.

Westermann's remark had knifed home; Cody remembered bitterly that this was the town that had insulted and humiliated Star – maybe even killed him if Doc Meadows was right. They didn't want the town ordinance enforced, so let them see what it was like to have a wide-open town. *To hell with 'em all!*

At the doctor's, Meadows met him at the door of the infirmary.

'He's unconscious. I'm going to have to operate, get that bullet away from the lung. It's chancy, but he will certainly die if I don't attempt it.'

Cody looked past the man's shoulder, saw Star's bandage and part of the dark, still face. He nodded.

'Do the best you can, Doc. He's a good Injun – one of the best.'

He went quickly to the livery, where he saddled his mount quietly and led it out through the rear door without any one seeing him. He tethered the animal in a lonely, dark place not far from the bank and found Meecham pacing like an expectant father near the side door.

'Where the hell've you been?' the banker snapped.

'Had a few chores to do. What's up?'

'I want you to guard the safe, starting right now. I know it's early but I'm prepared to pay double.'

Cody fingered the can of chloroform.

'Pretty generous, Abe. I earn an extra ten dollars for keepin' close to thirty thousand bucks safe for someone else, huh?'

Then a voice spoke from the shadows.

'There's a helluva lot more'n thirty thousand in there, Cody.'

Mel Ryan and Bill Ritchie stepped forward, cocked sixguns in their hands.

Meecham's eyes bulged. 'What the devil is this, Mel?'

'Let's go inside,' Ryan said easily, showing the banker the side door. 'You can leave that Greener, Cody. You won't be needin' it.'

'Nor anythin' else,' said Bill Ritchie bleakly. ' 'Cept a headstone!'

CHAPTER 13

THE LONG GOODBYE

Meecham was shaking when they reached the giant safe. The keys on their ring rattled and clinked as he took them from his pocket at Ryan's command.

'You can't get away with this, Mel!' Meecham bleated. 'Think about it, man! You're robbing the bank with the *sheriff* as witness!'

Ryan laughed. 'He don't count.' His voice hardened. 'Neither do you.'

Meecham's face was bloodless now, his breathing heavy and wheezing.

'You'll give him a heart attack,' Cody said.

'So? Heart attack, bullet. He's dead either way.' Meecham's legs went rubbery and Cody steadied him. Ryan smiled. 'Small price to pay for fifty thousand bucks.'

The banker was incapable of speaking but Cody said:

'Fifty? Abe told me twenty-seven thousand.'

Ryan laughed. 'That's the payroll – the rest is what

Brother Jake took in all them nasty hold-ups that've been happenin' up in the hills and along the trails the army uses. Scared the pants off everyone, specially the army!' He cut off abruptly, flicking his eyes from one man to the other. Meecham was too frightened to think straight but Cody suddenly nodded in understanding.

'Your brother uses the men they send him! Army trash, servin' out their sentences at lonely Fort Randolph, organized by the commandin' officer into a gang of thieves to hit every payroll, bank or stage that carries cash. Bein' the only army post up there, he'd be told in advance when money was passin' through his area. Ryan, that was one good idea!'

Ryan sneered. 'You're dumb, Cody! You still don't see it. Sure, Jake made thousands in them hold-ups but he couldn't get it out of Randolph easy—'

'So he slipped it in with an army payroll and sent it here where you were waitin'. But how could he be sure the payroll would be comin' here for the stopover?'

Ryan flicked an eyebrow at Cody, encouraging him to think it through. And the sheriff did.

'I get it! All those hold-ups were along routes normally used by the army. Must've made 'em mighty nervous about usin' those trails come payroll time. Till Brother Jake suggested they send the money in to Randolph in the supply wagons, a little at a time, then he'd ship it down here with an escort to wait for the train to Fort Worth. A lot safer than usin' the old regular trails where outlaws were active, eh?'

Mel Ryan frowned. 'How you know about Jake havin' 'em send it in a little at a time with his supplies?'

'You don't get it, do you, Mel?' Cody gave the rancher back his own words. 'Star and me intercepted an army letter to Jake acceptin' his idea, even tellin' when the payroll would be comin' to American River.'

'Judas, Mel!' exclaimed Bill Ritchie. '*That's* why Cody and the Injun came here! They aimed to steal the damn money, too!'

Ryan laughed, shaking his head. 'And the town made him sheriff! Put him right at the safe's door! Oh, Cody, it'll be a shame to put a bullet in you! But it's gotta be done! Hell, I could've used you no end.'

'You must've got a mite shaky when Bo Bantry and his gang held up Abe's bank. If the army figured it was that easy to raid, they could've changed their mind about bringin' in the payroll.'

'But you stopped Bantry an', with a sheriff's star, hung around till the money arrived. You must've reckoned it'd be mighty easy for you to get your hands on that cash.'

Meecham stared in horror at Cody. 'You – were going to rob my safe all along?'

'Was workin' on it, Abe,' Cody admitted. 'But that combination lock bothered me.'

'Hell, that's fake,' Ryan said and Meecham snapped his head around.

'It was to be connected up later when some parts arrived from Europe. But how d'you know that, Mel?'

'Jake has his contacts. All right, Abe. Shake out

them keys and get this door open. Time's a'wastin'. . . .'

Meecham found some courage and refused. Ritchie poked him hard in the spine with his sixgun. Ryan backhanded the banker, sent him staggering. Ryan's gun hammer cocked and Meecham's eyes bulged.

'I can just take the goddamn keys and do it myself, Abe!' Ryan reminded him. 'Give yourself another few minutes to live and oblige me, huh?'

The banker's fear returned and he began shakily to sort through the keys on the ring. He had trouble fitting them in the slots and Ryan, impatient, cuffed him savagely.

'Leave him alone,' Cody said and saw the murder in Ryan's eyes as the man swung the gun on to him.

'I don't really need you at all, Cody!'

'Let me do it, Mel!' Ritchie said eagerly. 'I owe this bastard plenty!'

'Wait till we get the safe open and the money out. Town's rowdy but a gunshot might bring someone sniffin' around. Abe, you got that damn key in yet?'

Meecham steadied himself, slid the first key home then the second. He was sweating profusely as he looked at Ryan.

'The keys are supposed to be turned simultaneously.'

The rancher jerked his gun barrel at Cody and the sheriff moved alongside the banker, grasped the right hand key.

'Whenever you say, Abe.'

Meecham licked his lips, nodded, and they turned

the keys, hearing the big tumblers slide back into their slots, kept turning until the keys came up hard against the stops.

Ryan stepped forward, grabbed Meecham's shoulder and sent him stumbling into a cupboard against the wall beside the safe

'All right, Cody. Swing the door open.'

Cody grasped the large nickel-plated handle, braced his feet against the bottom frame and felt his shoulder muscles crack as he threw his weight into it. But the door opened surprisingly easily and he stumbled with the suddenness of it. Inside were metal shelves containing all the bank's private papers, a few security boxes, cartons of files, some canvas bags marked with the American River National Bank's name in stencilled letters, secured at the top with slim chains threaded through brass eyelets in leather strips and padlocked.

Resting against the rear wall on the floor was an iron-bound chest, heavily padlocked – four locks altogether – and stamped 'US ARMY'.

'How the hell we gonna fit that on a pack-hoss, Mel?' Bill Ritchie asked, sounding slightly breathless.

'We open it and take out what we want, you damn fool,' grated Ryan, breathing a little faster, too. He grinned as he took four keys from his pocket. 'Brother Jake, thorough as usual, got copies.' He turned to Cody and Meecham. 'Well, boys, I guess you've outlived your usefulness.'

Ritchie smiled as he lifted his gun and put it on Cody. And in the sudden, hushed silence, they felt the first trembling run through the strengthened

145

hardwood floor beneath their feet. They even swayed slightly.

'What the . . . ?' Ryan looked confused.

They all felt it. Cody said calmly:

'Could be an earth tremor – recollect readin' this once used to be earthquake country . . .'

There were muted rumbling sounds from outside now and Ryan snapped at Ritchie to go take a look. The man came back, eyes bugging out, trying to swallow, his mouth suddenly dry.

'It – it's a stampede! Main Street's full of steers! They're wreckin' everythin'!'

Ryan laughed. 'Durango's surprise! He said he'd keep the town busy and have our good sheriff here runnin' his butt off!'

He stared at Cody who kept his face blank. *If he had been working alone, with the safe open, the stampede would have been ideal – taking the town's attention while he got out with the payroll. Now, all it had given him was perhaps twenty seconds of extra life while Ritchie checked it out . . .*

The guns were coming round again.

'What's that I smell?' Ryan said.

'Might be this,' Cody said, bringing out the can of chloroform. He had managed to work the cork out and jerked it in a spray towards Ryan's face.

The gun made a deafening crash as it went off within the confines of the safe and Ryan screamed as the chloroform burned into his eyes. He clawed at his face, moaning, and staggered. Ritchie had been too surprised to react at first, but now he swung up his gun, as Cody splashed more chloroform in his direction.

It didn't take Ritchie in the face but it soaked into his shirt and splashed on to his hand. The shock of its coldness before it started to burn made him gasp and he looked down to see what it was, gun wavering. Cody lunged, thrusting Meecham out of the way.

The banker fell, striking his head on the metal shelf-frame, opening a gash in his temple and knocking the consciousness from him. Cody stepped over him and hit Ritchie, but Ryan, still stumbling about blindly, crashed against him and the blow only glanced off Ritchie's jaw. Cody struck his head on the edge of the door, and was momentarily dazed. Ritchie fired wildly, the bullet tearing into a cardboard box rammed with files as he turned and ran for the door. Cody straightened, the room swimming, as Ryan lunged down the short passage to the side door too, still tearing at his face. He seemed to have forgotten about the smoking gun he held in one hand.

By the time Cody reached the side door it was swinging open and he could hear the full roar and thunder of the stampede of 2,000 trail-spooked steers, no doubt hazed along by Durango and some of his men – those he hadn't yet let loose on the town to create as much havoc as possible.

Some trail bosses just loved the chance to square things with stuffy towns that tried to curtail their 'fun'. . . .

A bullet tore splinters from the door-frame and Cody dived headlong through, rolling in against the bank wall. Another bullet screamed off the red brick, dust and chips stinging his face as he grabbed at his

Colt. Then he saw the Greener where he had propped it before entering the bank. He snatched it up and brought the shotgun across his body.

He glimpsed the muzzle flash – the sound drowned out by the noise of the stampede – and it showed Bill Ritchie crouched by the corner of the building across the alley. The shotgun roared and kicked into his body as he pulled both triggers. Ritchie's body was picked up, hurled against the building, a large semicircle of chewed splinters exploding from the frame. He tossed the empty shotgun aside, got to his feet and started after Mel Ryan.

At the end of the alley he skidded to a halt. Main Street was like a stream in flood, only it was dust-backed, bawling, red-eyed, horn-tossing cattle instead of water that filled it from side to side. Awning uprights splintered and the frames collapsed, spilling streams of shingles. As they poured down on to the backs of the cows following those that had caused the crash, the beasts panicked even more and began trying to climb over each other. One crashed through a store's plate-glass window, bellowing in terror and pain.

The din was terrific. There were men shouting, and shooting, frantically trying to turn the steers. But there was nowhere for the cows to go except straight ahead. A few veered off into alleys. Others just kept ploughing on, confined by the stores and houses of Main Street, smashing through everything in their path.

A couple of riders forced their way through but they looked like trail men to Cody and would no doubt be actually increasing the raw panic of the terrified beasts.

Then he saw Ryan.

The man had risked his life to get to a horse trough, plunged his face in again and again, desperate to kill the burning, blinding pain of the chloroform. He lifted his head, gasping, water streaming from him, right at the edge of the bawling cattle. One actually shouldered him aside and Cody marvelled that the horns hadn't raked the rancher.

Ryan stumbled clear and saw Cody in the swaying amber light of a porch lantern. Cody saw what looked like shreds of skin blistered from Ryan's face. The man's teeth bared in hate and he triggered two fast shots at Cody who leapt back from a wildly swinging set of horns, heard them crunch along the bank's front, gouging the brickwork. One of Ryan's bullets ricocheted above his head and he slammed two shots in return, tried to find a place safe from the stampede where he could trade lead with the rancher.

Ryan, heedless now of any danger from the steers, focusing his overwhelming hate on Cody, lunged forward, his gun in hand, firing again and again, hammer clicking on empty chambers as he kept on working the trigger. Cody beaded him, and then suddenly Ryan was gone. No screams. No throwing-up of arms, just – gone. His hat surfaced briefly, leaping across dusty red backs, torn, shapeless and stained darkly, and then the herd thundered on without faltering for a second.

Cody lowered the hammer, took one last look at the wreckage caused by the stampede and which was still occurring as the beeves surged on relentlessly through the town and fleeing people. Then he turned back down the alley towards the bank.

He smiled when he entered, closed the door after him, then moved Meecham's still unconscious form a little. He picked up the four brass keys on a ring which Ryan had dropped when the chloroform had burned his eyes.

Cody walked into the giant safe and knelt before the army chest, sorting out the keys, hands shaking a little.

Ted Scanlon was surprised to see that the leader of the posse was Big John McKenna – a sheriff's star pinned to his vest.

They looked a grim and determined crowd, armed to the teeth. *If ever they catch up with Cody . . . !* he thought.

'That Cody's bronc I see in your corrals, Scanlon?' barked Big John, pointing to the sorrel everyone knew to be Cody's.

'That's right, McKenna. I was just thinkin' of ridin' into town to get someone out here but didn't want to leave Rose and Cathy alone after what happened.'

'And what did happen?' Big John was mighty unfriendly, his face still showing fading bruises and cuts.

'Well, Cody rode in here last night – early hours of the mornin' to be exact – put a damn gun on me and told me to saddle up two of my fastest broncs.'

'An' you done it?' Dandy Grills growled.

Scanlon swivelled hard eyes to the saloon man.

'What'd you expect me to do when he had Rose and little Cathy in the parlour under his gun, damnit?'

Westermann, face battered and swollen, spat.

'He wouldn'ta hurt the kid! He saved her before!'

'You can say that, Dallas, but Cathy's *my* kid. Cody might've saved her in town but now he's the one that's desperate. Yeah, I gave him two fast hosses and he took some grub. I was worried he was gonna shoot us all, he looked so damn wild . . .'

'He near killed Abe Meecham, stole the army payroll,' McKenna explained. 'Durango swears it was Cody started the stampede that just about wrecked the town so as to give him time to get away. He shot Bill Ritchie to hell and someone saw him tradin' lead with Mel Ryan before Mel got trampled somethin' awful. I guess I can b'lieve you was scared for your family, Scanlon.'

'You *can* believe it!' said Rose from the porch, holding Cathy in her arms. 'He – he seemed a different man altogether. He frightened all of us very badly!'

She seemed to give Cathy a slight shake. The little girl sniffed.

'Cody-man had a gun,' she said. 'He was mean-looking. I was scared!' The child sniffled again.

That was enough to convince the hard-eyed posse.

'You see which way he went?' demanded Big John McKenna.

Scanlon pointed south-east.

'That way. But I think he might swing north once he gets to Rimfire Ridge. He asked me one time about the country between here and the Indian Territory, wanted a lot of detail.'

'He did, huh? Well, he'd have plenty of outlaw friends to help him in the Territory if he made it.'

'One of the hosses he took has a chip outta the left arm of the off-side front shoe,' Scanlon volunteered helpfully. 'Leaves a distinctive track.'

McKenna nodded curtly

'Obliged, Scanlon. We'll push on . . . after we take a look around.' He smiled thinly. 'You got no objections, have you?'

Scanlon spread his arms.

'Help yourself. You're loco if you think I'd hide Cody after what he pulled. I was partial to him for what he did for Cathy, but now! Makes it worse, him leavin' his pard into the bargain.' He shook his head slowly. 'I don't hold with that kinda stuff.'

McKenna grunted. 'The Injun's good as dead anyway.' He detailed four men to search the barn and other buildings, even the house.

'Don't you traipse mud and dirt across my clean floors!' Rose said snappily and the two men due to search the house wiped their boots self-consciously.

The search produced nothing and no sign that Cody had ever been here.

McKenna scowled. 'We'll get movin'. There'll be a good reward for recoverin' that payroll and these folk can use a few extra bucks after the way the town got wrecked.'

No doubt that was meant to take the edge off the townsmen's anger; a lot of it would be directed at Durango, and his crew, despite Cody being blamed for the stampede.

Scanlon stood on the porch with Rose and Cathy and watched the riders turn and cross his pastures in the direction he had indicated – and where he had laid tracks in a false trail that would lead the posse away from the direction Cody had really taken.

'They must be desperate to make Big John sheriff.'

They turned at the voice and Rose said sharply:

'Stay in the shadows in case they see you!'

Cody stepped back a pace, holding his rifle down at his side now. He watched the posse's dust-cloud for a time then grinned at Cathy.

'You were a very convincin' little actress, Cathy. I'm sorry I had to ask you to tell a lie.'

'I didn't, Cody-man. You did look mean when you were talking about Mr Ryan. I really was frightened!'

Cody's grin widened. 'Well, I'm sorry about that too. Right smart little cookie, you got there, Ted. I'd best be pushin' on in case they turn back. Wouldn't want to get you folk into trouble and I got a long way to go if I'm swingin' down to El Paso.'

'Will you ever come back?' Rose asked softly. Scanlon glanced at her sharply, took Cathy from her arms and carried his daughter back into the house, tickling her and making her laugh.

'I'd come back if I thought you were waitin',' Cody answered the woman.

'I'd wait, Cody,' she said even more softly.

'I'm an outlaw and a thief, Rose. It's army pay I took and some's from what Ryan's brother and his gang stole.'

'I know. But all that money is usually insured. No

one will lose except Jacob Ryan and his outlaws and the insurance companies.' She smiled, cheeks dimpling. 'I *know* they can afford it. I worked in one of their offices in Denver for a time.'

Cody regarded her soberly.

'I've got to wait in El Paso for a spell – or across the river in Juárez. I gave my word to Star I'd stay long enough to be damn sure he's not gonna make it before I move on. I guess I'll have worked out somewhere to go by then.' He shrugged awkwardly.

'Are you asking would I come down to Juárez if you sent for me?'

'Somethin' like that – but we wouldn't have to stay there. We'd have enough money to go just about wherever we wanted. Like California.'

'That's a long way from Ted and Cathy,' she said slowly.

'Yeah, I guess. I dunno if Ted would want to give up his spread, but it'd be OK with me if he tagged along – and little Cathy, of course.'

'Well,' she said with a sigh, 'it's something to think about, isn't it.'

Their gazes locked and after a short time he nodded.

'Yeah.' He sounded disappointed, but he knew she was right. Such decisions could not be made on the spot, not when they would have such far-reaching sequences. 'Look for a letter from someone named "Chris Hatch" sometime.'

Despite his impatience to be away, Cody waited until dark. By that time Scanlon had the two horses saddled, provisioned and ready to go. Cody was using

154

the buckskin for his mount right now, but later would change with the bay that carried the supplies, and the money taken from the army chest. The money was evenly distributed in canvas sacks and one square leather box with a buckled strap.

Cody buried this box in the grain bin where Scanlon would be sure to find it. He rode out into the night. He kept to shadows; Scanlon had muffled the horses' feet with pads of burlap. He passed through the darkness like a ghost.

There was still a chance a mean, vindictive type like Big John McKenna might have left a man in the timber to watch the ranch. It bothered him a little that there might be repercussions for the Scanlons if the posse truly suspected the rancher had helped him.

But he made it into the hills safely and started the long, slow climb, taking wide-swinging zigzags as the rocky trail rose more steeply. He kept just within the timberline, dropping down where necessary, picking his way amongst boulders. It was dry ground and the horses made a fair swirl of dust as they skidded because of the slope's steepness. Even a little haze spreading across the brilliant stars would be suspicious enough but there was little he could do about it. Hours later, he made camp amongst a heavy pile of rocks butted up against a bank where wind-blown conifers grew, leaning outwards. Their branches would disperse smoke from any fire he built; it was chill at night and in the early mornings in these high hills. But he decided to forgo the warmth of a fire, staked out the horses securely, made his bed against the sacks containing the moneybags. He slept with rifle to hand and sixgun loosened in the holster, ready for any trouble that might arise. . . .

Yet he wasn't aware that an intruder had entered his camp until a gun barrel prodded him roughly in the side, bringing him out of the blankets, snapping taut like a spring, the rifle coming up and across his body.

A gun stock slammed against his skull and knocked him flat, head buzzing, a Fourth-of-July sunburst behind his eyes. He didn't take long to get back enough vision to see the man sitting on a rock, rifle casually covering him while he puffed at a pipe.

'Almost made it, din' you, Cody.'

'Durango . . . ? Wondered what'd happened to you, why you weren't with the posse.'

'Hell, that lousy town wanted me to pay for the damages caused by the stampede. Big John was smart, talked 'em into givin' him the law badge, and took the posse after you. He'd've got his hands on that money somehow and left me flat. But I managed to get away and watched Scanlon's; knew you just had to be there, so waited you out.'

Rubbing at the swelling now on his head, Cody smiled a little.

'Did you have to tell 'em *I* started the stampede?'

The trail boss chuckled.

'Wasn't she a humdinger? You ain't popular anyway. But never mind that. I'm more interested in what you got outta that bank. Knew Ryan was up to somethin' there. Miserable cuss paid me just five hundred bucks to get my men tearin' up the town while him and Ritchie got to the bank safe. But they're both dead now and you're the one got away with the loot.'

'What makes you think I got any money?'

Durango sighed, tapped out the pipe's dottle, ground it into the dirt with his boot, and stood up. He jabbed the rifle at Cody's face but the man jerked his head aside, although the foresight tore a thin red line across his cheek.

'We'll have no beatin' about the brush, Cody! You got that payroll and I want it.'

Cody blinked, swaying a little, making out he was dizzier than he really was.

'We could split it.'

The trail boss snorted.

'Man, I ain't interested in splittin'! I been pushin' beef up and down the trail since the war's end. I've got stone arrerheads in me, at least one Yankee musket ball, knife-scars, busted bones and arthritis that ties me in knots. I want life to be *easy* from now on. That money' gonna do it for me. Now, step aside!'

He jerked the rifle barrel and Cody knew he was a breath away from dying. *So he had nothing to lose!*

He rolled, snatching his Colt and shooting across his body as Durango's rifle whiplashed. The trail boss slammed back three feet, struck the rock he had been sitting on, twisted violently and hung there, his rifle clattering as it fell.

Cody sprawled, trying to prop himself up on one elbow, feeling the numbness from the hammer blow that had struck his side, knocked him back on to the blankets. His hand came away wet and red, dripping. It hurt to breathe.

'Damn! An' me with a thousand miles still to go.'

But he had incentive now, in the shape of all those greenbacks – and the hope that Rose Scanlon might yet come and join him.

Such thoughts helped drive him to a sawbones this side of the Border who he knew would care for him – for a price. Just as well, too, because the wound was worse than he had first thought and he was forced to stay at the cabin belonging to the doctor for two weeks in order to recuperate. So it was almost a month after tangling with Durango before he eventually rode into Juárez.

There had been two more attempts to take the money on the trail down, but he had killed both men. One was Big John McKenna under a shaggy beard and a lot of trail dirt. He no longer wore a sheriff's star and died cursing Cody's name.

Cody decided he was getting too old for this kind of life . . .

He found a small adobe shack outside of Juárez with a brush awning where he could sit and watch the sun set across the Rio, sipping a little tequila and lemon-juice. A cur dog had come with the shack and attached itself to him after he tossed it a couple of chicken-bones one time.

Weeks later, one balmy evening, he was attempting to write to Rose Scanlon, wondering whether, after all, he had any right to expect her to share his life even if he did 'retire'.

Hell, he'd ask her anyway: there was *something*

missing from his life since Star had failed to turn up. He knew the Indian must have died: he'd have made it some way if he hadn't. Maybe Rose could help fill the gap. He lifted his pen, poised, searching for words that sounded right.

The dog was lying beside his chair, sleeping, he thought. But now it sat up, growling quietly into the sundown.

'Easy, feller, no need to chase rats now you get decent grub . . . go back to sleep.'

But he tensed as something moved in the hard shadows under the trees and a tall shape stepped out, trail-dusted and gun-hung, clothes hanging loosely on the raw-boned frame. His hand dropped to his gun butt.

Then a familiar voice asked: 'Are you rich yet – paleface?'

Cody stood, grinning, going to meet this apparition from the past, hand outstretched. Life didn't seem so empty after all.

'California, here we come!'